# Moral Adjacent

Sean Boling

Published by Sean Boling, 2020.

MORAL ADJACENT

**First edition. January 6, 2020.**



ISBN: 979-8224512652

Written by Sean Boling.

# CHAPTER 1

A handful of people get to know us any better than a college admissions officer. We take offense as we submit to them, railing about how much more there is to us than what's on an application, but peer judgment is no less swift, maybe even more shallow, and an honest look back tends to reveal our profile as destiny, regardless of any spikes or dips in the trend. Even when someone makes a giant leap in status from middle school to high school, we can find some evidence of what was to come, an underdeveloped talent or body. Same for those who fall into teenage obscurity after a run of childhood popularity. There was something unsustainable about their juvenile dominance. They wore a hat well, or were bold when riding a bike. Maybe they become one of those seniors who don't list any accomplishments under their name in the yearbook. Nothing but blank space where the clubs, activities, sports, and witty quotes are supposed to be. They don't submit a senior portrait for their picture, either. They let the yearbook staff use their ID photo: messy hair, rumpled hoodie and all. And for the most part, you can guess who the blank-space seniors are going to be when they're in elementary school. The sorting happens early.

Esmeralda Lockhart hung out with those who were bound to have long lists and snazzy photos. Her friends were not the most popular, but they were the most driven, and they were not letting a chance to finally look good in a picture pass them by. Their list of endeavors would be accompanied by a pose from their photo shoot, maybe that one in the vineyard looking back over their shoulder, or the one on the train tracks with the water tower rising behind them, or that shot from the ranch series cradling a baby goat, or maybe the one in front of the fountain at that really big winery. Something at sunset to symbolize a beautiful wrap to a brilliant four-year career. Esme and her crew would joke about these things, but their cracks allowed a little truth to seep in, particularly during junior year, their last chance to impress the objects of their validation, a final plea to Stanford, USC, or a top-three UC.

Which is why Esme took Journalism junior year. She was a great addition to the staff, but putting out the best possible edition of our paper every month only interested her in that it meant we were likely to continue our run of state and national awards, not because she had any passion for the subject. She was a theatre kid who played the flute every fourth Sunday at a local church she didn't attend because she didn't have time to commit to the school marching band. She mixed in some Future Farmers of America her freshman year by raising a lamb to sell at the fair because Drama and FFA is a combination they probably don't see very often on a college application. She ran with the cross country team sophomore year while working at the nursery school for the Early Childhood Education program since she had raised that lamb and figured how much harder could toddlers be? Every summer she took dual enrollment classes through the local community college to clear space in her fall and spring schedule for more classes. And through it all she maintained one of those grade point averages higher than a 4.0 because of all the AP and Honors courses she aced.

It was performance art based on a long line of artists who came before her, and who had been rewarded for their display. Some of the seniors who played their part well were receiving early decision notifications around the time Esme first pitched an idea to our editor, a story that was innocuous on its surface, but ended up rewriting her outlook on life.

A couple of the seniors were going far away, to Brown and Cornell. One got into Claremont McKenna, closer to home. Several more were rejected and had to wait to hear from their other options, along with the rest of the anxious horde, after the new year.

Our editor-in-chief, Daisy, was part of the academic pack that hunted for colleges with Esme. While some in their circle, like Esme, had chosen to build their applications on variety, Daisy was the type who built hers on steadfast dedication to a single pursuit. She took Journalism as a freshman, grew smitten with the subject, and became the first junior to be named managing editor since the paper started raking in awards during the fifteen years that Mr. Hawley had been serving as faculty advisor. So when Esme said her story was about the local hospitality industry, it's easy to imagine Daisy taking it in a more investigative direction than Esme intended.

"Its effect on our economy?" she hoped.

"Kind of," Esme hedged.

"How so?"

"What the jobs are like."

"The working conditions," Daisy lit up.

"Kind of," Esme smiled.

Daisy sighed.

"It's not fluffy," Esme reached across Daisy's desk and squeezed her forearm. "I've got some depth in mind."

"You're not going to ask them what celebrities they've waited on?"

"That was my airport story."

"I know."

"Come on. That was fun. People liked it. To think our cute little airport has all that star power passing through it."

"Private planes are the only kind that land there. There's bound to be some famous people in them now and then."

"But we named names."

"Very hard-hitting," Daisy deadpanned.

"You ran it," Esme reminded her.

"And I don't want to run it again. What's your hospitality angle?"

"I want to find out if working at the higher-end, chic hotels and restaurants is better than the average version, or if it's the same old job dressed up in wine money."

Daisy appeared to enter a temporary meditative state and took a bite out of her Nutella sandwich. She liked the pitch, but knew Esme hated taking lunch in the Journalism room and wanted to make her wait.

"I like it," she announced during the tail end of her bite as she brushed her hands together to free them of crumbs.

"I already know who I'm interviewing," Esme added what she assumed was good news. "Sage Lee works at the Brasserie-whatever downtown, Blake Thomas works at the hotel with the Italian name I never pronounce correctly, and my Dad knows pretty much everyone who works at the dive diners and cheap motels."

Daisy wasn't enthused.

"What?" Esme addressed the lack of energy.

"Does it always have to be easy?"

"Easy?" Esme suddenly seemed very intent on staying put and sacrificing lunch to stand her ground.

"I don't mean everything in your life," Daisy backtracked. "I mean for the paper. I know this is just another way for you to bat your eyes at your favorite colleges..."

She held up her hand as Esme moved to object.

"We all do it," Daisy assured her. "I get it. We've all got our eyes on the prize. But I've got all my eggs in this basket. If this paper doesn't keep pumping out accolades, I'm gonna need like a fifteen-hundred on the SAT to make up for it, or else I'm in for two years at A&M."

We called our local community college 'Harvard A&M.'

"What's wrong with having my sources lined up?" Esme lowered her defenses enough to focus on the pitch.

"Maybe nothing. But maybe there are better sources."

"Do you really think the story is that great?"

"I don't know. But I do know Blake Thomas is turning into that guy who graduated but keeps going to the prom for like five more years, and I can probably tell you what Sage Lee is going to say."

Esme jumped on board and imitated a rapid, teen-girl accent.

*"It's like, pretty cool, I guess. Good money."*

"*But, like, soooo many people talk behind my back,*" Daisy piled on in the same speedy lilt.

"*And my boyfriend gets, like, soooo pissed when guys hit on me.*"

"Soooo..." Daisy dropped the caricature. "You can kind of see what I'm saying?"

"Yes," Esme bowed her head. "I will merely use them as a way in, and be on the lookout for others once I'm there."

"Your Dad's buddies ought to be fine."

They smiled at each other.

Daisy changed the subject to clear a path for Esme's escape from the Journalism room.

"Looks like Rafa didn't get into any of his early decision colleges."

"Maybe he did and hasn't told anyone."

"He would have posted a foot-long thank-you humblebrag to all those who helped him along the way," Daisy scoffed.

"Maybe those schools figured he wasn't going to accept their offer anyway, with an application like his."

"Or there's a point where you start to creep them out instead of dazzle them."

Esme was out of maybes but no more willing to accept Daisy's position in their latest stalemate over Rafa. She fled the stuffiness of the newsroom into the somewhat open air of the quad.

She spotted Rafa, which was not hard to do on any given school day, as he seemed to be everywhere. He was in her field of vision at that moment under the trellis that ran along the entrance to campus. She watched him from a distance, as she had since middle school. If they had been in the same grade, she would perhaps consider him a rival, like Gina Ruiz. She and Gina had been earning the same grades at the same time for six years straight, all the while scanning the landscape for any advantage to clinch the top spot in the class rankings. But Rafa was a year above Esme, so she had put him on a pedestal during his seventh grade year from her sixth grade perch. He unveiled the power a student could wield if they were strong enough to impress teachers, charm staff members, and converse with parents as though they were peers, all while withstanding the razzing from his actual peers and maintaining a fair number of friendships with them as he waged his craft.

Her study of him that afternoon in the quad was accompanied by the crunch of her Sun Chips, the sound symbolizing in her mind the shock of her idol being denied by any school fortunate enough to receive an application from him. He wore no signs of distress over his rejection. Esme would be devastated if that happened to her, more than likely refusing to leave the house for at least twenty-four hours. She made a mental note to not tell anyone if she decided to apply for any early decision schools, and also suspected that Rafa's rejection letters were nothing but a rumor as she watched him roll through clique after clique as if running for office as the incumbent in a non-competitive race. He glided from some football players to some members of the jazz ensemble to some kids Esme didn't recognize. He appeared to have a personal handshake routine for each one, and even more impressive: something to talk about.

"Barf," she heard Irma's voice over her shoulder.

"Wrong," Esme corrected her as Irma came around to her side and tried to steal one of her chips but couldn't get her hand in the bag smoothly enough.

Esme gave her one.

"Thanks," Irma crunched.

"It's remarkable," Esme went back to her Rafa-watching.

"So fake," Irma maintained.

"Who cares if it is?"

"Are you kidding?"

"Think of the skill and talent involved. He remembers whatever little thing binds him with each person or group. That's not just memory. He had to listen carefully to learn those little things. He has to care on some level."

"About himself."

"They get something out of it."

"Tolerance," Irma quipped.

Esme tried not to laugh.

"You need a ride somewhere after school?" she distracted herself.

"Which direction are you headed today?" Irma weighed the invitation.

"The Tuscany resort hotel, assuming my source confirms."

"Interview for the paper?"

"Yup."

"Anything else?"

"I'm recording some wind for the sound board in the theater."

"I thought Robin was doing sound design."

"She is, but her wind sucks. It's her doing an imitation of it into a microphone."

Emse imitated Robin imitating the wind.

"Sounds more like the roar of a crowd," Irma said.

"There's a place on the undeveloped side of Goldfinch Road where the wind comes through just right. Jostles the tall grass in the meadow."

"Can you do that first?" Irma asked. "Push your interview back a few minutes?"

"I suppose."

"You can drop me off at my Mom's cousin's friend's place on the way."

"That's a new one. Where?"

"The Enclave."

Esme dropped her shoulders and raised her eyebrows.

"You know someone who lives in The Enclave?"

"My Mom's cousin's friend."

"Is he a doomsday prepper?"

"She's a she."

"Oh my God. They have women out there?"

"My Mom's cousin's friend."

"I guess they need them for breeding after the apocalypse."

"Can I get the ride?"

"Hell yeah," Esme enthused. "I've always wanted to go there but was afraid I'd be lined up in the scope of a rifle. Now I have a reason I can give them when they holler 'What are y'all doin' here?' through a slightly-open window."

The bell rang signaling the beginning of the end of lunch.

"Maybe you can do a story about how it's not really like that," Irma suggested.

"Not if it's not really like that. Where's the fun in that?"

"You parked in the cul-de-sac?"

"I am."

"See you there."

The Enclave is only two minutes outside the city limits, and two minutes is about how long a person can have a conversation with Irma's mother before they start to look for a way out, including Irma.

Irma almost always went somewhere after school other than home. Esme almost never asked why. When she did, she could hardly believe the answers, and hardly contain her disbelief. Sometimes Irma offered her mother's whereabouts unprompted, possibly to prove that her mom wasn't weird after all, or maybe to show how unique she was. It was difficult to tell. Her mother's actions had no scale. There was no high and low end. Every activity was an outlier. But it wasn't hard to tell that Irma was being protective of her.

"Mom's looking for free pots," she mentioned as they passed the last vineyard before The Enclave.

"Free pot?" Esme asked for clarification. "Or pots?"

"Pots, plural. As in pottery."

"That's good."

"She doesn't smoke pot anymore. Unless she has money. Which is why she doesn't smoke pot anymore."

"What are the pots for?"

"To break and turn into art."

"Like a collage or something."

"Something."

"Where does she find free pots?"

"She goes on that local website where people try to sell their beat-up old shit and when she goes to pick it up, she drives them crazy before paying so they just give it to her. They should be giving it away, anyway. She shows them the light."

Esme slowed into the turn at a dirt road with a homemade plywood sign staked to its side. The wood had grayed with age, along with the once-black stenciled letters that read "Enclave, CA", making the name hard to see.

The sign's haphazard construction foreshadowed the rickety brood of homes that surrounded a courtyard of dirt.

"Does your Mom know you're here?" Esme asked with genuine concern.

"Yes," Irma sighed. "She bounces around a lot, but she keeps track."

"I didn't mean anything by that."

"I know."

"Well, I meant something. But it has to do with this place, not your Mom."

More cracks and holes and chips revealed themselves the closer they drew to the homes.

"They're good people," Irma assured her. "Most of them."

"Most of them?"

"The not-good ones aren't bad. They're harmless."

"If you say so."

Esme looked at her phone as she pulled to a stop in the center of the splintered circle.

"There's no service out here," Irma told her.

"I'm checking the time in case I have to testify."

Irma backhanded her in the arm and climbed out.

"Thanks for the ride," she said through the open door as she slung her backpack over her shoulder.

A weather-beaten woman in brown corduroy overalls and an untied terry cloth robe walked through the door of a house that seemed to be made of the same plywood used for the sign. A black and white pot-bellied pig followed her out and stood by her side. The woman waved at them from where the front yard would be if there was one.

They both waved back.

"I love you," Esme told Irma.

Irma smiled.

"Don't overuse that word," she warned before shutting the car door.

Esme took no offense. The warning was based on a conversation they had many times, inspired by a moment when Irma told Esme she loved her as they said their goodbyes between third and fourth period.

"I love too many things," she added right after she said it, and Esme laughed.

Their AP Lit teacher happened to mention days later how many more words the English language has than any other, a dozen synonyms it seems for every word, yet we claim to love everything, from our grandparents to pepperoni on our pizza. The two friends took that notion to heart and periodically came up with ways to differentiate the kind of love they felt for each other to other kinds of love. Esme would say "I love you more than a warm chocolate chip cookie, but less than my future children" and Irma would say "I love you more than my kaiju action figures, but less than my second husband who will be the true love of my life after a failed first marriage."

Esme watched Irma walk to the robed woman, who hugged her, while the pig looked on. A pang of envy took her by surprise. She put the car in gear and rolled out of the dust, back in the direction of civilization.

During the drive, she distanced herself from the unexpected warmth she witnessed by considering the contrast between the property she just visited and the one she was heading toward. What stood on each plot was the vision of an ambitious person. The difference in what those visions ended up looking like, she decided, was money. One had it, the other did not. While she reached her conclusion, the moneyed version came into view: a Tuscan-yellow, two-story, two-hundred room resort rising above acres of wine grapes planted by its visionary.

The interview went about as she and Daisy had predicted.

Blake led her into the courtyard with its fire pits, plush patio furniture, and full-grown olive trees that had been trucked in and planted with backhoes. They sat in the center of it all, a symbol of how Blake perceived himself. But he had little to contribute other than observations that anyone could make, whether they worked there or not, regarding how beautiful the place was, and how expensive.

"How would you compare this job to the one you had at Motel 6?" she asked him.

"I don't know," he shrugged. "I worked there for, like, a week."

"Oh..."

"Is that a problem?"

"Well, my article is about comparing one type of hospitality job with another, and when Karina told me you worked at the motel before you worked here, I thought, 'perfect.'"

"Karina..." he repeated the name in a mutter.

"Did you guys break up?"

"No..." he leaned back in the fluffy chair and looked up at the sky framed by the walls of the resort. "Yes. Maybe. I don't even know anymore."

Esme was determined to avoid that subject. She pressed him with some follow-up questions about the job, how the wealth on display and passing through may affect the working conditions. Blake seemed to gather in real time that he might be able to capitalize on networking opportunities that the guests represented. He could make connections with some of the regulars, score a bunch of seed money, and invest in a sandwich or pizza franchise, a place where he could hire teenagers and hang out with them for the rest of his life.

She imagined him pursuing that realization too hard in the coming weeks, battering visitors with an aggressive charm, and getting fired. She asked if anyone else might be available to speak with her, and Blake grew even more excited as he led her inside and introduced her to the manager of the restaurant, who had worked in other hotels and restaurants over the past decade, and with whom Blake seemed to think he had a chance.

Her name was Trudy, and she grinned at Blake's attentiveness that he coated with a flirty varnish. Esme couldn't tell whether her smile was appreciative or charitable. After he excused himself to "let you ladies talk," Esme couldn't resist the tug of her own biases and played to the possibility she was merely tolerating Blake.

"He's adjusting to life after local hero worship," Esme explained.

"Excuse me?" Trudy said while adjusting herself in a chair that sat across a table from Esme in the empty dining room.

She said it innocently enough, but Esme grew flustered at the thought of misreading the moment.

"Oh," she backpedaled. "He was a really good football player at our high school last year. The man. All that. Probably why he keeps dating this girl who's younger than him, so he can go to the winter formal and the prom and take his mind off being a regular student at A&M."

"A&M?"

"Our local junior college. It's what us snotty, arrogant, Type-A students call it. Harvard A&M. I'm sorry..."

She waved her arms as though trying to erase the past ten seconds.

"I'll stick to questions about the restaurant business."

"No worries," Trudy assured her. "Sounds like my ex-husband. I was the second girl still in high school he dated after the one a year ahead of me graduated."

Esme exhaled with relief and commenced the interview.

She liked the feel of it, more conversation than interrogation, and her feelings were confirmed when Trudy offered to exchange numbers in case either of them thought of anything else that may add depth to the piece. They swapped phones and tapped in their contact info.

When Esme reviewed her notes later on, certain lines appealed to her beyond their relevance to the story she was tasked to write. She especially liked the part where Trudy lamented the shallow labor pool of applicants with high-end service experience, as it spoke to what bothered Esme about her hometown: it had the amenities associated with the wine industry, but was still small. Most everyone else saw this as a strength. The chamber of commerce designed every promotional campaign around the "Small Town Charm, Big Time Wine" aesthetic. But to Esme, it was a trap. Fine for the retirees who flocked there, or the tech professionals who worked from home, but a beautiful dead end for someone her age. As limited in opportunity as it was in size, but filled with luxurious short-term bait that could trap a young person into staying to their long-term detriment. She could imagine coming back someday, but in triumph. She wanted to lounge by the labor pool rather than tread water in it.

# CHAPTER 2

Esme thought the hardest part of following her plan to craft the ultimate college application would be sacrificing lead parts in the school plays. She had dominated the local youth theatre company as a child, likewise conquered the middle school program, and had people predicting future stardom as she entered high school, the freshman prodigy starting for the varsity team.

Filling out the audition form the first time was indeed difficult. Writing "ensemble" under "desired role" felt like a hostage situation. The character she really wanted to play was held captive by her ambition, by the sprawling course she had mapped for herself. But as she played her part in the background on stage, her star was rising off stage, which made it easier to brush off the thump of regret she experienced when the lead actors would misinterpret a line or sing off-key. What used to mean everything to her was now "just a high school play," the mantra she would repeat when the envy creeped up on her. All that mattered on her college application was that she had done it, not how much nuance or verisimilitude she brought to the role. And the acclaim she earned on her new path was much more widespread. The compliments she received from drama were limited to people who saw the shows, a rather small and particular slice of the community. Her expansion into multiple areas led to an exponential increase in praise.

"Is there anything you can't do?" was her favorite pat on the back.

"Sports," was her usual reply for a while, until she joined the cross country team. Then she modified her modesty to "Kick, throw, or catch a ball of any kind."

The spring musical junior year, the year she checked off the journalism box, presented the greatest challenge to keeping her eye on the prize. She had dreamed of playing Roxie Hart in *Chicago* since she was ten years old, when she was introduced to the role by one the teenagers she worshipped in the youth theatre company, who would give Esme a ride home and blast the soundtrack in her car. The day her teen idol told her she was born to play the part went from being a pleasant memory to a frustrating one when the high school director made the *Chicago* announcement. Esme wished out loud to many a friend that it was scheduled for the following year, her senior year, when applications would already be sent and her GPA was under less pressure. But they weren't there yet, and meanwhile the SAT and ACT were that semester, along with the usual assignments to whup, flute solos to play, pre-school children to encourage, and perhaps another story or two to write for the paper. Foregoing her dream role would be the truest test of discipline in the march toward her real-life dream. And pretending she wasn't bothered by watching someone else butcher Roxie would be the performance of a lifetime, even if only she knew it.

Well, she and her friends. She would wind up venting to them quite a bit, she imagined.

And her Mom. She would have to hear about it.

Maybe her Dad, though paying attention was difficult for him.

She liked the girl who got her part. She was a perfectly adequate actor, a serviceable singer, and excellent dancer.

"Like most dancers," she couldn't resist adding as she described the first day of rehearsal to her Mom. They had both arrived home around the same time and were standing in the kitchen passing a bag of goldfish crackers back and forth.

"Most of them are really good?" her Mom wasn't sure what she meant.

"Well, that too," Esme clarified. "The percentage of dancers who are good dancers is way higher than the percentage of actors who are good actors. But no, I mean dancers usually aren't very good actors. Too broad. Not believable."

"Shouldn't be a problem in a musical," her Mom shrugged as she dug into the bag.

"Watch," Esme took the bag from her. "And plug your ears. She'll be screaming her lines."

She offered the goldfish back to her Mom, who refused with a wave.

"You should have auditioned for the part," her Mom said.

"You know the plan," Esme rolled up the bag and put it aside.

"I don't always understand the plan," her Mom looked through the cupboard for dinner ideas.

"But you know what's up with extracurricular activities these days. You've complained about them. Crazy levels of commitment. It's like choosing a major. I probably wouldn't get the part, anyway, because I haven't devoted myself enough to the drama department. Nobody is allowed to try different things. You have to try to be a star in one thing. But meanwhile, the colleges say they want variety, curiosity."

"It's your choice in colleges I don't understand," she turned to the refrigerator, the cupboard having failed to inspire her.

"I'm not going to work for a university," Esme reminded her. "I'm going to use one."

Lupe Orozco-Lockhart preferred to go by Dr. Orozco. She claimed it was because her hyphenated name was too long, not because of anything associated with her husband's name. And she said that the "Dr." in front of her name prevented any confusion as to whether students should address her as Ms. or Mrs. or Miss. She used to work at the kind of university her daughter wanted desperately to attend, but now worked at the state university forty minutes away. Esme was too young to remember the move, and Lupe withheld many of the details as to why it happened, other than to say a meteor may not have killed the dinosaurs, but it killed her career in academia. She was at the wrong school for the kind of research she was conducting. She had a better relationship with people in her field on other campuses, those who were also skeptical of the meteor theory. When support dwindled within her department to the point of impasse, she decided to not only switch schools, but focus more on teaching and less on research. The cattiest of her former colleagues translated this as a euphemism for more work and less pay.

Lupe claimed this made her happier.

It also laid the foundation for her bewilderment years later over Esme's adoration of an institution she found petty and venal, but which most of all had scorned her.

"Revenge," Esme growled with a conspiring grin.

Lupe smiled back, but with a slow head shake while she continued to survey the fridge.

"If you choose your professors wisely," she said, "you can get as good an education, maybe better, at a CSU or a community college."

"It's not about the education."

Lupe closed the fridge and gave Esme her full attention.

"No?"

"It's about prestige, connections, networks..." Esme rattled off. "It's getting what you pay for."

Her mother inhaled and leaned back on the counter.

"When you get to whatever hot shot school you settle on," she said. "And I don't doubt you'll have a choice, for I am utterly confident in you...don't be too freaked out when the disappointment comes. It comes for everyone, usually in the first year. The question is how you handle it. Push through? Pull the plug? Change course?"

"Oh, I know how I'm responding," Esme declared. "If for no other reason than to keep you from saying 'I told you so.'"

"I wouldn't do that."

"You would think it."

"No, you would think I was thinking it."

Esme tried not to smile, but with limited success.

"Either way," she straightened her face, "Strong motivation."

"Don't let your pride be your guide."

"Don't talk to me about pride. You're against my plan because of your pride."

"I'm not against your plan," Lupe lifted her arms in absolution. "I just wish you'd have some fun."

"I have fun."

"When?"

"With my friends."

"What about drama, journalism, music, cross country..."

"Jobs. Bullet points on a resume."

"That's sad."

"That's life these days, Mom. It's the world we live in."

"And whose fault is that?"

Esme hesitated.

"That's right," Lupe reacted as though she had responded.

"It's not only the colleges," Esme followed up on the answer she hadn't actually voiced. "The colleges are responding to demand, and the demand was created by everyone asking us to start planning our future when we're in sixth grade, to get in the cage and fight for a spot. Does a university that goes from a seventy-five percent acceptance rate twenty years ago to a five percent acceptance rate do that by itself? And then all these old farts have the nerve to say my generation is soft and weak. I'd like to see them try to get into the colleges they got into way back when. They just went. Coasted right in, nothing to it. Try that same routine nowadays. See how that works. Wouldn't get a sniff, not even from Cal-State Where The Fuck Is That. But they don't care, because they got theirs, then blew up the bridge. Well, I'm gonna beat them. I'm gonna play their game and dunk on their ass."

Lupe finally smiled the way Esme hoped she would earlier when she had tempted her mother with academic revenge.

The approving look didn't come easy, spreading over the course of several seconds from begrudging to proud.

"Should we order out?" Lupe asked.

"Sure," Esme agreed. "What about Dad? Is he out back with the birds?"

"No. I think he's in negotiations. I saw his van around the corner."

He preferred to park away from home when he needed to set the voices straight.

He refused meds because they dulled emotion, and he needed his emotional intelligence at full strength to mediate their demands, which were often coded.

If a voice told him to leave his family because they didn't love him anymore, for example, that meant he needed to show his family more often how much he loved them. Once he learned how to interpret their taunts for his own ends, he found them rather helpful. He claimed they originated on the job, back when he was a licensed contractor and he would talk to himself during long stretches of humdrum to help pass the time. When he lost his business, that trauma triggered another one from his past he had tried too hard to forget rather than face. His own voice was drowned out by those of his father and his grandmother, who took turns manipulating him, often by disguising themselves as other voices.

"We don't have our tie-breaker vote," Esme noted regarding her father's absence.

"Maybe we won't need it."

"We won't if you're in the mood for Golden China."

Lupe appeared to convince herself she was. She pulled out her phone.

"I'll pick it up," she offered. "You probably have homework."

She placed their usual order.

"Thank you," Esme hugged her.

"It's a five-minute drive," Lupe joked, aware the embrace had nothing to do with dinner.

They held on for what felt like enough time for the food to be prepared.

"Any catering gigs coming up?" Her mother asked to help ease their disentanglement.

"Still too early," Esme answered. "The weather isn't quite springy enough."

As she went upstairs after her Mom left, she paused to look through the window alongside the staircase to see if she could spot her father's van on the adjacent street. It used to belong to a large plumbing company that swapped out its old fleet. Her father had painted over their corporate logo, but it still loomed faintly behind his handmade scrawl that read "Warren Lockhart: Handyman at Large". He also ran a homing pigeon business, but that was strictly through word-of-mouth.

She couldn't see any part of the van. Instead she caught sight of her neighbor from across the street arriving home from his shift at the tire shop. He had graduated two years earlier. They used to play as children until their age and gender made it awkward. Since then, she had watched him grow more sullen as he bounced from one unsuccessful attempt at acceptance to another, never quite getting the hang of skateboarding, then football, then dirt biking, then fixing cars, consumed by anger he never expressed but always wore.

"Now that I think about it, he may have been my initial inspiration for the plan."

"The Plan," Daisy held up her hands as if framing the words. "Sounds like a fad diet."

"Or what you're supposed to follow in some cult," Irma added.

"He was such a sweet kid," Esme ignored them.

They sat at a table in a corner of the taqueria down the street from school before she had to go back for rehearsal.

"I think it sounds more cultish when she calls it The Path," Daisy said.

"I call mine The Track," Irma confided.

"I wonder if he applied anywhere," Esme speculated.

"Besides the tire store?" Daisy asked.

"I don't remember him," Irma said. "You never pointed him out when he was still in school."

"Never thought to," Esme admitted. "We never spoke once he hit fifth grade. I tried to say 'hi' every so often but he wouldn't make eye contact."

"Does he own a gun?" Daisy asked.

"Stop," Esme dragged out the word. "I feel bad for the guy. He scares me, but for a different reason."

"He didn't get denied by any colleges," Irma assured her. "Even if he did, he still could have gone to one. State, A&M, whatever."

"It's not that," Esme stared at the last rung of the tortilla that had been wrapped around the burrito she ate. "More like, is that what happens when dreams don't come true? Any dreams?"

"Did he have any?" Irma asked.

"Any that don't involve violence?" Daisy quipped.

"I don't know ," Esme answered. "He had imagination as a child."

"Everyone does," Daisy claimed.

"Relax, Esme," Irma cut to the chase. "You're getting into pretty much every school you apply to."

"That's only Part A," she said. "Part B is the financial aid offer. I'm more worried about that now."

"There's always something," Irma shook her head.

"Easy for you to say," Esme countered. "You're gonna make it rain."

"How do you know?"

"Does your Mom even have an income?"

"Your Dad works under the table," Irma reminded her.

"But my Mom does pretty well. And they're still married."

"Okay," Daisy stopped them. "Y'all are about one more sentence away from saying something really awful."

"You're right," Esme said to Daisy and then turned to Irma. "I'm sorry."

"It's The Path talking," Irma said. "I get it."

"You know I love you," Esme confirmed.

"How much?" Irma asked.

Esme thought for a moment.

"More than this taqueria and less than life itself."

"I have a solution," Daisy declared.

"We stopped arguing ten seconds ago," Esme reminded her.

"Was that an argument?" Irma wondered.

"I mean when it comes to paying for college," Daisy said.

"Why didn't you tell us before we almost argued?" Esme chided her.

"You remember Audrey Oates?" Daisy asked.

"She was hot," Irma recalled.

"Very hot," Esme agreed.

"Well, I ran into her the other day…"

"I thought she was up at Oregon or Oregon State," Irma interrupted.

"She was."

"I don't like this story already," Esme commented.

"It has a happy ending. She's transferring to UC Santa Cruz next Fall. Okay?"

"Now you spoiled it," Irma teased.

"That's not the best part. And it's not the point. Remember, this is about money for college. Which Audrey didn't have enough of. She was running out by the end of sophomore year. So she floods the town with job applications and makes the rounds for interviews. While she's waiting her turn to talk to the manager at some artisan, craft, organic, farm-to-table breakfast place, she notices this girl sitting by herself at a table checking her out. Giving her some real long looks. And according to Audrey, this girl was hotter than she was. When she's done with the interview, which lasts like a half an hour, she sees the girl is still there, like she's been waiting for her. She walks by the table, and the girl asks how it went. She says it was okay, and the girl asks if she's trying to pay for college. She says yes, and the girl asks if she'd like to hear about a scholarship that provides a full ride for a full year..."

"Oh God..." Irma covered her mouth as though listening to a ghost story.

Esme shushed her as Daisy continued.

"Turns out there's this old rich guy who pays a new college girl every year to accompany him places and spend a designated amount of weekends at his house. There's a contract and everything. It has an official name, the Charles Fucking Weirdo Johnson endowment, whatever his name is. But it's not on any scholarship websites or anything. Obviously. Part of the deal is the girl has to recruit new candidates toward the end of their year, and that's what this girl was doing."

"I'm not hot enough," Esme sighed.

"Me neither," Irma commiserated.

"Aw, come on," Daisy encouraged them. "Don't sell yourselves short."

"If Audrey Oates is the standard?" Esme pointed out.

"She didn't do it," Daisy reminded them. "That's why she's headed to UCSC next year. Maybe the dude aims for an Audrey and ends up with someone like us. Classic negotiating technique."

"Assuming there's that same dude in whatever college town we end up in," Irma said.

"So was it Oregon or Oregon State?" Esme feigned interest.

"If we laughed at each other's jokes, I would totally be laughing now," Daisy said.

They took a break to finish whatever was left on their plates that still interested them, and head to the beverage station for refills.

After returning from her trip with a full glass, Esme noticed a text from Trudy, the manager of the restaurant in the Americanized Tuscan villa resort.

"Hmm…" she hemmed as she read it before providing a summary to the table. "That's sweet. One of the housekeepers at the hotel gave Trudy a letter to give to me. I guess she saw me conducting interviews and wanted to get in on it, but doesn't speak much English and was self-conscious."

"I'd say 'stop the press' if that edition hadn't already come out last week," Daisy tried to stab her last few kernels of rice with a plastic fork.

"Maybe a follow-up," Esme suggested.

"Oh," Daisy stopped her stabbing. "That reminds me. I meant to run this by you, Esme, but spaced out. As for a follow-up, how about a piece on the new hotel going up on the way out to the golf course? Build on the hospitality theme."

"Is there an angle?"

"Not really. Straight reporting. What goes into a project like that, who's involved. Very little effort on your part, but we could still maybe run it as a feature with the right pictures. Just the kind of thing you're looking for."

"Let me run it by Irma."

She looked at Irma.

"Should I do it?"

Irma took a sip and looked away.

"All right, then. Sign me up."

Irma snapped back to attention and looked aghast.

"Damn," Esme deadpanned. "Did I misread those signals?"

"Whatever…" Irma pouted.

"Well," Esme lowered the curtain on their performance by running a napkin over her section of the table and crumpling it onto her plate. "I want to head out a little early so I can stop by the resort before rehearsal."

"To be clear," Daisy said as Esme rose from her chair. "The hotel construction story wasn't acting. That's real."

"And I'm for real doing it," Esme assured her. "Can you give Irma a ride?"

"Yeah," Irma turned to Daisy. "Can you give me a ride?"

"Depends," Daisy hedged. "It's not out to some ranger station or an abandoned summer camp, is it?"

"Nope. Just home."

"How refreshing," Daisy exhaled.

"Mom's planting some turnips and could use some help."

"I'll drop you off down the street."

"Relax. I meant I'm going to help her."

"Bye," Esme made her escape.

"Break a leg," Irma called after her.

"At rehearsal," Daisy added. "Not the hotel."

Esme appreciated the chance to see Trudy again.

She seemed to enjoy her life more than anyone else Esme had met who had not gone to college, and Esme felt she needed to know more people like that.

The letter was in a sealed envelope.

"I wrote your name on it," Trudy said as she handed it over. "Dorothy only knew you as the newspaper girl."

Esme laughed and thanked her. They small-talked for a minute before Esme promised to deliver a copy of the current edition with Trudy's quotes in it as soon as she could.

"Maybe Dorothy can make it into the next one," Trudy suggested.

"I pitched a follow-up to my editor," Esme said, which was sort of true. "We'll see."

After saying their goodbyes, she was curious enough to open the letter before reaching her car. She walked slowly along the gravel path lined with columns of Italian cypress trees that ran parallel to the parking lot, and walked slower with every sentence until she froze.

*My name is Dorothy and I am from the Philippines. I was promise work in America by company they lie. They say job pay much, but money is much less. Then they take out a lot money for place to live, but I live in tiny place with too many people work in hotel. Then company take out money for things not true. They watch us always. They threat to our family. They threat to send us to deport. I am sorry my letter take long to write. One lady of us she speak more English than us. But I do not know any trust. I use computer in little room next to lobby help translate when nobody see me. I am sorry to ask help, but I am sad and scared. I hope maybe girl at newspaper help. If yes, please write letter back and leave under green pot with lemon tree inside next to bocce ball place. I understand if no. Thank you.*

Esme read the message twice.

After the second time, she looked around, scanning the spaces between the cypress trees for a housekeeper watching her from a window, or peering at her from around a corner, like what must have happened during her last visit. She saw nobody. She remembered Blake regurgitating a line about the resort grounds being designed to create a sense of privacy no matter where a person walked. At the time she blew it off as propaganda. Now she was a believer. But instead of privacy, she thought of it as isolation. The imported trees towered over her and caught a light breeze she could hear, since she was standing still and the gravel no longer moved beneath her feet.

# CHAPTER 3

Friends and teachers told Esme they had never seen her so quiet. She would use her Dad as an excuse, say that he was having a harder time than usual. She knew he wouldn't mind. Really he was striking some pretty good deals with the voices of late. She was the one distracted from the inside. The voices were her own, and they had some strong opinions.

Nobody else knew about the letter. She hid it in her room, where she was spending a lot of time in order to avoid her parents. She didn't want them to notice her silence as well, and she couldn't use the Dad excuse, so when she would emerge in a haze, she blamed it on homework.

There was truth to the homework defense, but not for the usual reasons. She understood the assignment. Completing it was the challenge. She wanted to help, but didn't know how. If the company that the housekeeper worked for really was threatening her and her family, she didn't want to do anything rash and put her in any danger. She hatched a variety of plans and imagined everything that could go wrong with each one. Her frustration led her to decide she needed more information. She didn't know this woman. She had never seen her. Maybe the situation wasn't as bad as her letter made it out to be. Maybe Dorothy was not of sound mind, and this was nothing but an attention grab.

During her third night of turmoil, Esme finally grabbed a pen and paper and wrote a simple note that would be easy for Dorothy to translate. She considered writing it in Dorothy's language, but read more about the Philippines and discovered there were a lot of dialects. A closer look narrowed the likeliest possibilities down to two. Tagalog is the most common on the home islands, but many who leave to join the massive Filipino international workforce speak Ilocano, which set up her first question:

*Do you speak Tagalog or Ilocano?*

She had three more: *Where do you live? How do you get to work? What time do you work?*

She left it at that. She didn't want to make any promises or sound too encouraging.

On her way to school the next morning, she stopped by the resort. The bocce ball court was in the back of the building next to the pool. Activities were designed to be outside the center court so as not to interfere with its serenity. Nobody was using the pool in the morning chill of early spring, and Esme assumed hardly anyone ever played bocce ball. After checking to make sure no one lurked in a window, she left her note under the lemon tree in the green pot.

Making even a small move in a moral direction loosened her up. She was her usual self at school, according to those who commented. Signs of Dorothy still appeared in her conscience, but when they made their entrance, Esme took comfort in thinking of the note she left, and the excitement of checking for a reply.

She waited two days in order to give Dorothy a chance to choose her words and time to deliver them.

The sun had set when she stopped by their drop spot after rehearsal. Two little girls were playing in the well-lighted pool. Their mother was bound in a bathrobe sitting on the front edge of a lounge chair. She grinned and nodded when each girl demanded the spotlight and expected praise for going underwater without plugging their nose.

Esme stood in the darkness beyond the reach of the lights and appreciated the scene for a minute. Her childhood felt so long ago, longer than she had lived. The voices gave way to splashing and giggling as the girls improvised a synchronized swim with their feet likely touching the bottom.

Esme's pulse rate climbed, which she took as her cue to check the lemon tree.

There was a note.

She made sure it wasn't her own work still sitting uncollected before bringing it to the car. She left her door open to keep the light on. Dorothy's answers mirrored the tone and brevity of Esme's questions.

She spoke Ilocano. She lived in the Riverbed Motel. A van drove her to work. She worked every day from 8:00 in the morning until 6:00 at night.

Her quick volleys read like a call to action.

Esme looked at her phone.

It was almost 6:00.

She closed her door and drove around to stake out the front of the building. She parked in the short-term lot that fed into the main driveway. The digital clock on the dashboard of her car read 6:03 when a plain white van that looked like its pink slip had changed hands many times pulled into the entrance and drove past her post to the loading zone that circled beneath the arched brick canopy. Her view of the front doors was obstructed by the van and its position between the arches, so she couldn't see who was getting in or out of the vehicle. After idling for no more than a minute, the van pulled away and drove back down toward the road. Esme started her engine as it passed. She knew where the Riverbed Motel was, so she kept a safe distance behind the van. It was the kind of vehicle people associate with kidnappers and car bombs.

The motel was six miles north in an unincorporated outpost of a town serviced by a single off-ramp. The dirty white van took to its wrinkled main street and blended seamlessly with the murky houses that were hard to imagine ever being new. The motel indeed backed up to a riverbed, as the name suggested, but was also by the freeway, which whizzed along its banks. Water rarely flowed over the bed except after a heavy rain, and when it did, the noise of the current was no match for the sound of the traffic howling above it.

Esme parked across the street from the motel, which was two rows of dingy, boxy bungalows facing one another. The van was parked in between the rows. The light mounted on each unit was dim and made identifying any details difficult. All Esme could see was someone, probably a man, sliding open the side door as the engine ran and four people, probably women, getting out and walking into the bungalow facing them. After the women were inside, the man holding the door of the van slammed it shut, walked around to the driver's side, and climbed in. He put it in gear, made a three-point turn to reverse course, and left the buildings behind.

The motel seemed more quiet than the rest of the town after the van was gone. The door to the bungalow was still open. Esme considered walking over and introducing herself to whichever one was Dorothy, but she thought maybe some of them didn't want to cause trouble, or were satisfied with the situation. Before she could decide if those were valid reasons to hang back, two men emerged from the open door, closed it behind them, and stood guard. She was somewhat relieved to have the decision made for her.

Someone banged on her passenger-side window, shocking the deliberation out of her.

"You're parked in front of my house!" a wild-eyed person with long gray hair shouted at her.

"Sorry," Esme breathed.

"What are you doing here?"

"Nothing."

"Nothing?"

She was fairly certain the person was a woman.

"I thought I knew someone at the motel."

She started the car.

"That motel is for vagrants and welfare leeches."

"Okay."

"Tell your friend to get a job!"

"Will do," she drove off and hung a U-turn toward the southbound freeway entrance.

Once her heartbeat settled back down to a healthy rhythm, she decided the interruption was for the best. She didn't want to create any friction between Dorothy and any of her co-workers. In her next note, she would ask if the others in the bungalow were okay with getting help.

"Are you Filipino on any side of your family?" she asked Daisy during Journalism the next day.

"Do you really need to ask?" Daisy was riveted to a computer screen.

"I don't know. There's a lot of mixed families around here."

"We're straight Mexican, as far as I know."

"As far as you know," Esme saw an opening. "Maybe you should ask around. You might learn something."

Daisy peeled herself away from the screen.

"Why does it matter?"

"I need a translator."

"Oh…" Daisy realized. "Is this about the housekeeper who left you that note at the hotel?"

"It is."

"Is there a story there?"

"Well…" Esme didn't want to reveal the situation until she had a plan. "Maybe. Mostly I'm trying to be welcoming. She's lonely. Far from home. We're exchanging letters. Like pen pals but we hand the letters to each other."

"Cute. You sure you have time for that?"

Esme was about to protest before Daisy cut in.

"Kidding," she proclaimed. "Why not use Google Translate?"

"I want to sound like a human being."

"I hear that. Well, even though I'm probably not Filipino, there's like a hundred other kids in this school who are."

"I'd prefer someone I know."

"Blake Thomas!" it dawned on Daisy.

"Come on…"

"Seriously. Filipino on his Dad's side."

"No, I mean 'Come on…anyone but Blake.'"

"He's not that bad. And he works at the hotel with her. Perfect."

"His Dad may not even speak her language."

"I'm positive he's first gen. Heavy accent."

"With the name Thomas?"

"It's really Tomas, with the accent on the 'mas.'"

Esme sighed.

"Maybe Irma has someone in her tree," she speculated. "It's a very mysterious tree."

"I love this already," Daisy enthused. "If we have some room in the edition after next, we'll give her some love."

"Gina's family is Filipino," Esme continued to consider other options in the interest of ignoring Daisy.

"Gina Ruiz? Your arch rival?"

"I know," Esme moped. "And they're hosting that student from Afghanistan. No way they give me a chance to build an international relationship of my own."

"Just give Blake a try."

Esme combed her memories for other possibilities, any friends who may have said or done something related to the Philippines.

Daisy changed the subject, as though she had cornered Esme with Blake.

"Have you started on that hotel construction project?"

"Almost," Esme joined her in the new topic. "I'm interviewing some intern after school."

"An intern?" Daisy wasn't pleased.

"They're a big company. We're a high school paper."

"An award-winning high school paper. Show him our website. See if you can get someone higher up."

Esme was again more preoccupied with Dorothy's plight than with her immediate surroundings, but since her thoughts regarding it were now purposeful rather than aimless, her inward gaze came across as focused instead of foggy.

For the remainder of the bell schedule she wrote various forms of the message she wanted to leave for Dorothy, and contemplated which one would translate best.

*Do the other women care if I help you?*

*Do the people you are trapped with want help too?*

*Is it okay with your roommates if you receive help?*

She had a couple dozen lined up by the time she was free to visit the intern at the construction site.

He wasn't in the office, which was a trailer on the edge of the plot. A letter-sized piece of copy paper with a message printed in 48-point font was taped to the door:

*Be back soon! Come on in and have a seat!*

*—Josh*

She suspected he used the sign whenever he was out on the site, as it was frayed around the edges. She did what it said and took out her list of options so that her imaginary version of Dorothy could judge them while she waited.

*Do the other people in the motel want help?*

*If I help you, do I need to help the others?*

*I saw where you live. Do the others mind if I help you?*

Esme continued to linger mentally on the variations even as Josh arrived and proved to be a living embodiment of a college path she had dreamed of trekking: a recent graduate of the UCLA engineering program, merit scholar who emerged with barely any debt, his foot in the door of a company his alma mater no doubt touted as the kind of place where their graduates end up, all while being cute with charm to boot. Charming enough that he took no visible offense when he wasn't having his typical effect on a young woman.

"My editor was hoping to score some time with someone a little higher up the ladder," she said after running him through the pat questions about the size and scope of the project.

He laughed in stride.

"What more do you need to know?"

"I'm not sure," Esme admitted. "She's really proud of our paper. We've won some national awards."

"Impressive."

"She would agree."

"I'll see what I can do."

"Great," Esme said as she gathered herself for an exit before realizing something.

"If I get an interview with one of these head honcho people…" she settled back into the chair and leaned forward. "What should I ask them?"

"Hmm…" Josh leaned back. "Maybe get a sense of what it feels like to manage a project this large. What stresses them out? How do they deal with it?"

Esme let go of her translation fixation for the first time since she entered the trailer.

"Why not ask them yourself?" she grinned.

"Mustn't show weakness," he made a mocking fist.

Esme likewise leaned back.

"You gave me your bio earlier," she said. "But never mentioned what exactly you do around here besides regurgitate facts for the local press."

"I inspect the site and nitpick," he confessed.

"You?" she raised both brows. "I would think that's what the big cheese does."

"Big cheese wants to be liked."

"That sucks."

"I don't have to say anything to anybody. He's not forcing me to be the bad cop to his good cop. I take notes and he keeps them in his back pocket, so to speak, for when he needs them."

"And when might he need them?"

Josh smiled.

"I don't want to speak for him."

"Get me that interview."

"Give me your number and I'll keep you posted."

"Keep me posted?" Esme snickered. "How many updates do I need? Either I get the interview or I don't."

"I can let you know when I'm about to ask him, how he reacts, how long it takes for him to decide, maybe start a countdown. You know, keep track of the number of days since I asked. Send you a daily reminder."

Esme held out her hand. He placed his phone in her palm and she tapped in her number.

She had never exchanged contact info with anyone other than friends and members of group projects for school, so she couldn't evaluate her flirting with confidence. But she felt proud of it.

So proud she didn't dread checking in with Blake at the resort. Her poised interaction with a professional young man in his early-twenties rendered amusing her drop-in with the boy in his late-teens who wore a name tag. She carried her notebook of possibilities with her and caught him standing around the valet parking station.

"Does your Dad know Ilocano?" she asked Blake without saying hello.

"What's that?"

"A Filipino language."

"He speaks the other one."

"Tagalog?"

"Yeah, that."

"Thank God," she practically shouted as she pivoted back toward the parking lot.

She heard Blake moan "What the hell?" and imagined the look on his face, then thought of something and spun back in his direction.

"Do you know a housekeeper named Dorothy?" she asked.

"Is she young?"

Esme exhaled and wrapped it in a groan.

"Probably not young enough for you."

Blake thought that was funny.

"I know Trina," he said. "And she talks to a couple of other young ones."

"You don't know their names?"

"Not exactly. But I'm pretty sure none of their name tags say 'Dorothy.'"

"Maybe if they were as hot as Trina you'd remember."

"Probably," Blake saw no problem.

She considered a withering comeback to call out his callousness, but called it off. All he would do is feel wounded and cast her as a bitch in the story of his life. She also thought she might need him if springing Dorothy required some muscle. So she thanked him for his honesty and rather than walking back to the parking lot, went forward through the hotel and into the courtyard to find a seat and rely on her phone to translate.

She burrowed into a love seat with billowing cushions and flipped open her notebook to the options. The high season was still weeks away, so she was one of two people on the premises on a late afternoon. The other was a grandmotherly woman fifty yards away in a cluster of patio furniture on the far end where a stone double staircase led to the second floor.

As she assessed the sentences scribbled on the page, Esme was guided by her newfound knowledge that according to the view from inside Blake's cave, Dorothy was neither particularly young nor beautiful. She reached the end of her list and sank backwards into the seat. The sky held a few isolated clouds in the part she could see within the square formed by the roofline. She surveyed the windows surrounding her and debated roaming the halls to see if she ran into Dorothy. The hotel, she imagined, was ignorant of the situation. If their blind eye was willful rather than innocent, she didn't want to cause trouble. Not until she knew her play. Besides, the idea of meeting Dorothy in person made Esme nervous. She wouldn't know what to say, nor how to say it.

She looked into her phone and translated some key words: "others", "care", "help".

She managed to construct a sentence that didn't satisfy her pride of expression, but seemed to convey her meaning.

Leaving it under the lemon tree produced the same rush of excitement as the first time, but as she walked away, her adrenaline was drained by a pesky sensation that what she really liked was passing notes. She felt as though she was stalling, maybe hoping the problem would resolve itself before she had to do anything.

Dorothy's response drilled into this blossoming guilt. Esme retrieved it on her way home from rehearsal the following night. It was her shortest note, but expressed a rising desperation, and at four words long, Esme only had to read it once to read it a thousand different ways:

*What is your help?*

# CHAPTER 4

In spite of all her contributions to the mockery of their local community college, Esme preferred to conduct her research in its library. It was still a college, with access to the same databases as other institutions of higher learning, and she felt more grownup when working there. She appreciated the university library even more, not only for its enhanced contact maturity, but for the fond childhood memories. She would hang out in its stacks while her Mom met with students in her office. After Esme enacted The Plan and started to reach for a college of her own, getting to her old playground took more time than she usually had to spare, so she typically stuck with A&M.

A variety of keyword searches led her to some articles that described plenty of situations similar to Dorothy's. The more helpful pieces moved into an explanation of how they happen. She was likely here on an H-2B visa, lured by a foreign recruitment operation. Breaking free involved an interview with a federal agency, where she could declare she was a victim of human trafficking and obtain a T visa. The feds would probably dangle the visa in exchange for her cooperation in an investigation of the organization that drafted her.

With a stronger understanding of the circumstances and the consequences, Esme was ready to open up to her friends about what was happening, starting with Irma.

She reconstructed the timeline of events as they drove to a catering gig at a hilltop winery on a sunny Saturday that seemed to signal the entrance of spring. Telling the story while dressed in their uniform of black pants, black neckties and white shirts had Esme feeling like a private investigator updating her partner on a case.

Irma listened with an occasional concerned groan or moan. She didn't say anything until the part about the motel where the women were being held.

"The Riverbed?" she gaped.

"I know," Esme commiserated.

"They'd be better off in the actual riverbed."

"That's why we need to get her out of there. Maybe the others, too. We'll see what she says."

"I know someone who works for ICE."

"You know someone who works in Immigration?" Esme nearly pulled over.

"Lives out at The Enclave."

"Is it your Mom's cousin's friend?"

"It's my Mom's cousin's friend's nephew."

Esme devolved into a sequence of gleeful noises.

"I know you want to hug me right now," Irma said. "But don't. Our life depends on it."

"Both hands on the wheel," Esme demonstrated.

They drove for maybe a half-mile before Esme cleared her throat into a follow-up question.

"This person who works for ICE," she said. "He's not, like, bananas or anything, is he?"

"Get off The Enclave already."

"I'd ask you that no matter where he lives."

"He keeps his job."

"I don't want him getting all jacked up and busting in on Dorothy when we tell him about her."

"Don't tell him anything," Irma sighed. "Ask him questions."

"Won't he get suspicious?"

"He's not bananas, he's...what's a non-crazy fruit?"

"A level-headed fruit?"

"A sober fruit."

"Not grapes," Esme gestured at the vineyards they passed.

"Pears," Irma decided.

"Yes," Esme agreed. "They're built like serious men."

"Pear-shaped men with briefcases."

"And long marriages."

"Long, sexless marriages."

The nod to sex made her think of Josh the Intern. She had not heard from him since they swapped numbers the week before. Maybe she misread their exchange and there was no subtext. He really did just want to notify her in the event of an interview with the Project Manager or Chief Architect. She was a beginner, after all, and beginners don't get lucky as often as they make mistakes.

The wedding they worked was filled with Joshes. Some were men, some were women, some were young, some were old, but all were versions of Josh who had something Esme wanted. They were guests, not employees. Someone filled their wine glasses for them. When a Josh filled someone else's glass, it was because they wanted to, not because they had to. It was a gesture of friendship, or power. Joshes stood on the lawn that encircled the tasting room and took in the spectacular view of the valley below for as long as they chose to. When someone interrupted their meditation, it was to have a pleasant conversation with them, or introduce them to another Josh. Esme was barely able to appreciate the sight, and when she had a moment to try, it didn't last long before she was told to bus a table or take a lap with a bottle of white in one hand and red in another to see who needed a refill.

After an especially frantic casing of the room to make sure everyone had a glass of champagne for the toasts and the first dance, Esme and Irma wound up next to each other on the customer side of the bar for a breather.

"Look at us hunched over and exhausted," Irma noted. "I feel like we should order something."

"Someday," Esme said, her eyes on the future.

"I didn't mean that as something to look forward to."

Esme's eyes shifted to the present. She fixed on the open doorway behind the bar that led to a storage room.

"Did I just see Rafa?" she wondered about the person who had walked past the opening.

"Quite possibly," Irma answered. "His family owns this winery."

"How did I not know that?"

"You knew they owned one."

"Yes."

"You just didn't know it was this one."

"What do they do, exactly?" Esme pondered. "Where does the money come from?"

"I don't know what started it, but at this point it's money making money."

He walked past the open door again, pausing this time to glance out at the proceedings.

"Should we wave?" Esme asked.

"Gosh, Esme, I don't know," Irma teased her.

"I don't want to bother him if he's busy."

"You sound like we're waiting by the stage door after a concert."

"Well..."

"He's not busy. If he is, it's by choice."

Rafa saw them before Esme had a chance to make up her mind.

"Hey!" he said a little too loudly and caught himself in light of the toast being made.

Esme and Irma waved with contrasting degrees of enthusiasm.

He walked through the door and entered the inner circle of the bar.

"I didn't know you worked for Chef Tanner," he gestured at their uniforms as he reached the spot in front of them in a loud whisper.

"Why would you?" Irma asked the obvious.

"He caters a lot of events here," Rafa had an answer. "I figured I would have seen you by now."

"We're the B-team," Esme explained. "Only called for big events. His pro staff gets dibs. Then it goes by seniority."

"Makes sense," he processed her account. "Our events tend to be more intimate."

He smiled at her and Esme wondered if she was misinterpreting another possible innuendo. She looked at Irma and caught the tail end of an eye roll.

So he was insinuating something.

She applied Irma's confirmation to Josh. Twice in a week, from older boys, one of them maybe even a man. She was more confused than flattered.

The toast ended and everyone applauded. Chef Tanner appeared next to them and asked them to help with the cake prep.

"Can I lend you a couple of our people instead, Chef?" Rafa cut in.

Tanner considered his offer, but Irma stopped him.

"It's okay," Irma looked at Rafa while throwing her voice at her boss. "We're here to work."

She guided Esme by the elbow toward the kitchen.

"See you later!" Rafa called after them.

They bickered over Rafa's offer when they could during their walk back and forth delivering plates from the kitchen to the cake that stood to the side of the dance floor. The ideal moment was the space between the kitchen doors and the edge of the crowd, where neither the guests nor Chef Tanner could see them, which lasted a few seconds at a time.

"That was pathetic," Irma said as they burst from the kitchen with their first stack.

"I wasn't going to count it on my time card."

"I don't mean you. I mean him."

"Rafa?"

"Of course."

They changed their tone as they excused their way through the guests and delivered the plates to the cake table, then resumed their talk after they had nudged their way clear on the way back.

"Throwing his weight around like that," Irma clarified.

"He was being nice."

"In the only way he knows how."

"I don't understand why you hate him."

"I don't hate him. I don't understand why you admire him so much."

"What's not to admire?"

They entered the kitchen and quieted down until they had retrieved more plates and brought them out the door.

"He's not relying on his money," Esme continued. "He's made himself into one of the best students our school has probably ever seen."

"What else is he supposed to do with all that time he can spend?"

"He could do a lot worse."

"I'll give you that," Irma conceded. "But maybe there's a middle ground between useless and obnoxious?"

The crowd was upon them again. Though when they broke away on their way back to the kitchen, they found they had nothing more to say on the subject, nor anything else to say to each other for most of the night.

Part of their disconnect was due to Rafa remaining by Esme's side during the cleanup, ostensibly to help, but primarily to chat. The content of their conversation was not suggestive. He was pleased to find her so well-versed on the topic of college, and not from the overheated angle that raged through their fellow overachievers. She was as informed as she was inflamed. And as informed as he was, she was surprised to find him indifferent, approaching their discussion with a skepticism that threatened to rattle her foundation.

When they were done with the breakdown and conducting a sweep of the grounds to check that nothing was left behind, she at last mustered the nerve to ask him about the early decisions, and whether he really was denied.

"I wasn't rejected," he said while tracking some patio furniture that had been dragged into haphazard groups around the lawn.

"I didn't think so," Esme was relieved. She joined him in the setting sunlight to grab some chairs as well.

"I'm not going," he followed through.

The chairs looked like wicker but were really wrought iron, so each one required both hands to move.

"You're not going to any of the early decision schools," Esme assumed.

"Nope," he grunted as he dragged one back to the patio. "I'm not going to college at all."

Esme lost her grip on the chair she had chosen and put her hands on her hips instead.

"You're what?"

"I'm not going to college," he repeated as he put the chair in its place and strolled back onto the lawn for another one. "At least, not next year."

Esme couldn't move, much less speak.

Her sudden stillness drew his attention. He looked over at her and she discovered that in addition to not being able to move nor speak, she also couldn't meet his gaze.

"I know that sounds insane," he approached her with caution, as though she may attack. "But hear me out."

He passed her by and stood in front of the hills that caught the low sunshine that skimmed their tops and splashed them with orange light.

From inside the tasting room, Irma saw him take his place in front of the spectacular backdrop and shook her head at his never-ending need for showmanship. She was tempted to call Esme back in to perform some made-up task, but was curious to find out the subject of his lecture. Besides, allowing Esme to conduct a recap for her would give them something to talk about on the way home and thaw the ice that had formed in the latter hours of their shift.

He presented his hypothesis about college, and how it informed his decision to take a gap year.

"It was founded as a way to keep the rich on top, and still has that purpose," was his argument. "But now that purpose is camouflaged as opportunity. The acceptance rates were way higher back in the day because only certain people could afford it. College was a luxury some treated like a boarding school, a place where they could send their little wastrels to try and shape them up. Didn't matter how worthless they were, so long as the family had worth. There were exceptions, occasional lower income students on scholarships they had to work their asses off to earn, but they were human shields held up to make the institution look like it wasn't an elite circle jerk. When studies showed a correlation between a college degree and earning power, anyone who thought about it for more than a minute realized most students already had that power before they attended college. It was their social class, not their degree. But a closer look showed that those random kids on scholarship, those red herrings meant to distract from the privilege at hand, did in fact gain the kind of social mobility we like to provide just enough of so that we can keep saying "What a country!". And the race was on. The rich had to work a little harder to get in, but with the right SAT prep courses, the right tutors, the right extracurricular activities, the right study abroad programs, summer programs, charity missions, they could swing it. They had the resources. Not only to get in, but stay in, which is often the real trick. Besides, a lot of them were part of the system extending loans to the people they were now competing with, so they could make money off the race they were running, win or lose. Not that losing is ever a real possibility. Not in the true sense of the word. Not for them."

"Them..." Esme meditated on the word with Irma as they drove back into town.

"He should have said 'us,'" Irma scoffed.

"I didn't know how to respond," Esme continued as they swung through the latest curve in the road. "The sun seemed to sink below the horizon right as he finished. Like he somehow timed his speech perfectly. And it was a speech. He's definitely rehearsed it, or memorized the bullet points. I'm not the first person to hear it, either. He's run it by anyone who asks him why he's not going to college next year."

"See?" Irma interjected. "Phony."

"There was some freestyling at the end. He kind of slumped his shoulders and gave me this droopy smile that was supposed to make him look humble. 'I know it's a lot to take in,' he said. He walked up to me and put his hands on my shoulders. 'And I'm not saying you shouldn't go. I've heard you're an awesome student. If you still want it when the time comes, then go for it. I simply want you to understand my decision, one scholar to another. It's hard to explain to most people. But you're not most people.'"

"Oh God," Irma fretted. "Did he make a move after that?"

"I was still too frozen. Maybe if I had been able to look at him."

Irma chuckled and they took a couple of curves in silence.

"How exactly does that explain his decision?" Irma wondered aloud.

"I don't know," Esme was equally perplexed. "He's going to invite me to one of his parties. Maybe I'll ask him then."

"Please tell me you can bring a guest."

"Oh, you're coming with me. I don't care what the invitation says."

"Invitation?"

"Text blast. Evite. Something like that. Nothing formal."

Esme's phone bounced around in the plastic well under the parking brake. She grabbed it and peeked. There was a text with no name, just a number.

"Great news," it said. "My auntie speaks Ilocano."

"Who is it?" Irma asked.

"I don't know."

She figured it out by the time they pulled in front of Irma's house.

"Blake?" she wrote back.

"Yeah."

"How did you get my number?"

"Daisy."

Esme sighed and said out loud, "I'll have to thank her."

"Who?" Irma asked.

"Daisy."

"It's Daisy?"

"No, it's Blake. Daisy gave him my number."

"Wow. Another older guy."

Esme wiggled her head, waved her off, and eye-rolled as she fielded another text bubble from Blake.

"What do you need her for?" he asked about his aunt.

"Translating some letters."

"They use the same letters we do."

"Not alphabet letters. The kind of letters you send. Texts on paper."

"Oh. Duh. Sorry."

"Can you send me her contact info?"

"Just send them thru me."

"I'd rather not."

"Why?"

"None of your business."

"It's my auntie."

Esme growled.

Irma laughed.

"Fine," Esme both texted and said out loud.

"Looks like we have a translator," she told Irma before writing to Blake, "I'll send you the first one soon."

"When?" he wrote.

"Good night," she replied.

He texted her a peace sign.

"Blake is your translator?" Irma smirked.

"His auntie."

They looked at each other for a moment before bursting out laughing.

Esme composed her next note to Dorothy with deniability in mind. She didn't know Blake's aunt, and knew Blake all too well. She chose her words carefully, leaving certain spaces blank in anticipation of her interview with Irma's contact at ICE, which took a day to arrange.

His name was Zack, and he no longer lived in The Enclave.

He had moved into an outbuilding behind a bar called The Drum Solo which barely stood on an acre of land along the narrow, winding highway that joined the wine country to the sea. The plot was a bit past the halfway point heading west, closer to the Pacific than the vines.

"Where do your Mom's friends find these places to live?" Esme asked as they rolled to a stop in front of The Drum Solo, which was closed, maybe permanently. "Is there an underground network of unusual rentals?"

"Word of mouth," Irma answered. "Bathroom walls."

Esme studied her to confirm the latter was a joke.

Zack greeted them as they came around the side of the bar. He looked like he worked in the woods behind his shed as a lumberjack, or a bigfoot hunter.

"I'd invite you in," he waved. "But not much room. And the bar is closed during the day. Sometimes at night if there's no band playing."

"Mmm..." Irma looked at The Drum Solo as they passed it on their way to the front of his rental. "Can't wait until I'm twenty-one."

She introduced him to Esme.

"Nice trees," Esme looked on the bright side as they reached his dwelling on the edge of the pine forest made possible by the ocean air.

"Better than The Enclave," he said. "I had to get out of there."

"Not enough trees?" Esme quipped.

"Too much family," he took her question seriously. "My Dad built that disaster, and my Mom and her side of the family won't let it go."

"Oh," Esme cringed. "Sorry."

"No worries," Zack assured her. "Getting out of there got me into some honest work. Or a steady paycheck."

"And what is it you do for ICE?" Esme seized the opportunity to start the questions.

"I'm in ERO."

Both Esme and Irma held for an explanation.

"Enforcement and Removal Operations," he provided it.

"Well that sounds...soul-crushing," Irma said.

Zack chuckled.

"Beats holding on to a dead dream," he maintained.

"Crushing the dreams of others?" Irma jabbed.

"You two are closer than I thought," Esme intervened.

"He was like a big brother," Irma recollected. "Or one of those young uncles. At The Enclave, at least."

"Then there was your uncle at the Vineyard Management operations," Zack reminded her. "And at the DWP..."

"That was an aunt," Irma corrected him.

"This whole county raised her," he said to Esme, who kept up the interview.

"What happens when you remove someone from a situation where they're being held to work off a debt?"

"What kind of work?"

"Let's say housekeeping."

"Not prostitution?"

"Does it matter?"

"It can."

"How so?"

"How soon we respond after the report is filed. The more dramatic the situation, the sooner we'll get our orders."

"How dramatic is manual labor trafficking?"

"Might take a while."

"As in…?"

"Weeks, maybe months."

"And what happens after you get your orders?"

"They're detained over at a center in Bakersfield and they wait for an interview to try and get their T visa."

"Okay," Esme thought that sounded encouraging. "And how long does that take?"

"Maybe a year."

Esme reared back and looked at Irma. If a tree had fallen over, it would have provided a fitting sound effect.

"A year?" she repeated.

"Maybe sooner. But that's what I would estimate."

"What's it like inside this detention center?"

"The name says it all."

Esme tried to process her next move.

"People think we're dangerous," Zack filled the pause. "Some rogue operation…"

He puffed out a dismissive burst of air as a prelude to his conclusion.

"We can't abuse power we don't have."

"Well," Esme said. "Thank you."

"Anything you'd like to report?" he looked at the ground and swept the dirt with his foot.

She considered his question.

He swept the dirt back in the other direction with his other foot.

"If you tell me directly," he said, "I can shave off a whole lot of that response time I mentioned. From weeks to days. Maybe even hours."

She watched him fuss with the dirt until he completed whatever he imagined he was doing with it.

"No," she decided.

Zack glanced at Irma.

"Don't look at me," she said.

"All right, then," he stopped fidgeting. "Hope that clears some things up."

"It does," Esme shook his hand. "Thanks again."

"Have Irma give you my number," he suggested before releasing his grip.

She nodded.

He told Irma to say hi to her Mom for him.

Irma launched another crack his way, and he may have responded, but Esme was no longer paying attention.

She was combining the disappointment of her conversation with Rafa with the disheartening wait time for an interview with Immigration and arriving at an answer that was ready by the time they reached the car and Irma asked her "What now?"

She waited until they were both sitting down and had shut the doors.

"I'm going to break this story in the school paper."

# CHAPTER 5

She could write the story, but it wouldn't accomplish anything without being published, and it wouldn't be published without Daisy's approval. She sought her blessing early in the morning, knowing she'd find her in the Journalism room before the first period bell rang, before anyone else would be there. Esme wanted privacy.

When she finished explaining to Daisy what was happening between her and Dorothy, and what she would like to do about it, they settled into a staring contest.

Esme blinked first, blinked several times in her search for any expression on Daisy's face, but Daisy spoke first.

"Is this a good deed?" she asked. "Or is this a cherry on top of your college application?"

"Why not both?" Esme asked back.

"God forbid we do anything because it's the right thing to do."

"All year you've been on me about giving my stories more effort, taking more chances, and now I've got this bombshell ready to drop, you don't want it."

Daisy threw her head back and stared at the ceiling.

"Can't you just call your ICE buddy and get her out of there?" she said upwards.

"Then there's no story."

Daisy threw her head back down.

"Wrong," she glared at Esme. "There is absolutely a story. Report on it afterwards."

"I don't want to report it. I want to investigate it. I want to break it. The minute I call ICE and the workers are detained, everyone will know what happened and it's fair game. Anyone can write that story."

"If you nose around while they're still holed up in The Riverbed, you could put them in danger."

"If I wait until after the fact, everyone responsible will have gone into hiding."

Daisy responded by nearly sliding out of her chair in frustration. She gathered herself and sat up straight before trying to set Esme straight.

"No," she spoke as if providing a gentle explanation to a child. "Everyone responsible will be busted when you call it in."

"Only the guys holding them," Esme insisted. "The real crooks, the people in charge, will disappear into a pile of paperwork. They'll start a new company with a new name and do it all over again with a new batch of victims."

"They're already hidden. And who has a better chance of finding them? You? Or a massive government agency?"

"Did that come out the way you wanted it to?" Esme smirked.

Daisy one-upped her with a smile, slackening the tension between them.

"You?" she tried again. "Or a team of trained professionals?"

Esme ceded the point, and crafted a peace offering.

"Remember what my contact at ICE told me," she said. "Even after I report the situation, it could take weeks, maybe months to respond."

She left out the part about Zack saying he could trim the lag time.

"So how about I call it in," Esme continued, "then investigate it in the meantime?"

Daisy measured her compromise.

"This issue is very personal to me," she narrated her consideration. "My great-grandparents were repatriated during the Great Depression."

"Repatriated?" Esme needed an explanation. "I don't remember learning about that in the Depression unit."

"It's never taught. Doesn't fit the New Deal mythology. One of the ways America got people back to work, certain kinds of people, was to deport U.S. citizens of Mexican heritage."

"Citizens?" Esme made sure she heard right.

"Citizens," Daisy nodded. "It's all well and good to hire people to dig holes. It's even better when there aren't as many to hire."

"How do you deport a citizen?"

"You call it 'repatriation.'"

"Did they stay? Did they come back? What happened?"

"Some stayed in Mexico, some came back, a lot of them never felt comfortable in either place. They bounced back and forth across the border in limbo. My great-grandparents were bouncy ones, and so were my grandparents, since they were kids and had no choice. My mother finally decided to stay on this side. She didn't have to deal with the original order, so she wasn't afraid of committing, wasn't as bitter. But the family was fractured. They're all descendants of U.S. citizens, but you wouldn't know it if you held up the family tree next to a map."

"That's terrible."

"Help this woman," Daisy pleaded. "Don't use her."

"I won't," Esme assured her, then felt compelled to clarify what she meant.

"Use her," she confirmed. "I won't use her. I will help her."

"Have you even met her?" Daisy asked.

Esme shook her head.

Daisy blew some air through her nose that could have passed for either a sigh or a laugh.

"I guess it doesn't matter," she apologized, since either interpretation of her blow was patronizing. "She'll always be far away, no matter how close she is."

Some students entered.

Esme acted nonchalant, nodding at them and thanking Daisy.

She critiqued her performance as she left the room. Her nonchalance was overdone. She may as well have been whistling while she walked, or saying "la dee da dee da" in a sing-songy voice. Her overacting was understandable. She wanted to keep the story quiet. It was big and important, and she wanted it to herself. But she was also a touch embarrassed. Daisy's doubts left a larger mark than her approval.

Esme submitted the final draft of her latest letter to Blake so he could pass it along to his aunt for the translation. Her language was guarded:

*I will report your case, but it may take some time for the agency to respond. While we wait, I will investigate your situation. Do you have any receipts you can send me? If so, please include them with your reply. Your co-workers will of course be included in the operation when the responders arrive. Are you going to tell them what is coming? I would like to be aware of how much they know as I proceed with my investigation. I have a human translator now, as you can see, so you can send me your next letter in your native language. Thank you for your cooperation, and your patience.*

Blake's language was less guarded.

"What the fuck?" he replied after she sent him the text of the letter.

"You couldn't just write WTF?" she texted back.

"OK. WTF?"

"Send it to your auntie please."

"What do I tell her if she asks what this is about?"

"Tell her what I told you."

"What did you tell me?"

"Think."

A pause paved the way to his reply.

"None of my business," he wrote at last.

"Winner."

If his aunt did say anything, Blake didn't share.

He forwarded her translation without further comment.

Esme transcribed it in handwriting during her tutorial period in lieu of the Calculus homework that she finished later when she and the rest of the ensemble had downtime at rehearsal, after which she deposited the letter under the lemon tree.

The morning after delivery, Daisy approached her before first period to check if she had contacted ICE.

"Yes," she lied.

Daisy had reason to be suspicious. Esme was no less ambitious than the day before. But Daisy didn't look her up and down, nor ask twice. She simply thanked her and sped away to her first class.

Esme had already withheld information about Zack claiming he could compress the gap between reporting a situation and action being taken. Now she had outright lied. She was no longer hiding the exception Zack offered. She was pretending to take advantage of it.

She thought maybe Daisy would cast a more skeptical eye her way during Journalism later on, but that also didn't materialize. Daisy's faith in her had Esme feeling remorseful and ready to rationalize her decision to delay the call.

It was best to wait until Dorothy responded, for example.

Or...compiling some intelligence beforehand would expedite the process when she did call.

How about: Dorothy would get that interview with the feds right away thanks to the work she was about to do.

And she had a direct line to Zack. She could bypass official channels and cut to the chase.

She was buying guaranteed time, that's all, rather than wonder when ICE would bust through the door and break up her story.

So even though she had not initially planned to stall, that became her plan the morning she lied.

Dorothy's reply provided another burst of motivation. It was a thick collection of papers that would not have stayed folded if not for the weight of the potted tree on top of it. The first page was her letter, the others were receipts.

*Thank you for your help*, she said, according to Blake's aunt. *I am not going to tell my co-workers anything. I do not trust any of them, especially the one who speaks a little English and Spanish. They may be spying for the company, or willing to betray any of us who try to break free. Innocent or not, they will all have to learn about the plan as it happens. As you requested, I have attached copies of the monthly bills they hand us instead of our checks. They list the fees they are charging us. I look forward to hearing that knock on the door. Sincerely, Dorothy.*

Her reply also provided Blake with some inspiration.

"Dorothy!" he wrote in a text that arrived right after he sent his aunt's translation. "Didn't you ask about her that time you asked about my Dad?"

"I asked you about a housekeeper," Esme texted back. "But not by that name. Sorry. Nice try."

Of all the lies she had been telling, this one bothered her the least.

Fortunately no more letters were necessary. She told Blake to thank his aunt, and to let her know she'd be happy to pay her or buy her a gift card. She hid the pages of evidence in the bookshelves by her bed, between two volumes of the Percy Jackson series, her favorite when she was a little girl.

She was free to conduct business.

Her first move was to find out who was in charge of the resort, not only management, but ownership. She checked the databases in the university library and traced its development from approval to groundbreaking to grand opening, and noticed the man most quoted and photographed was often referred to as the "majority owner". She searched for the full roster of investors, but as she suspected, hunting the names would have to be a more hands-on pursuit.

She didn't want to check with city hall too early in the process, as she figured some of the stockholders would have friends on the city council or in key offices. They would notice she was tailing them soon enough, but she wanted that to happen as a result of asking them questions, in person, not second-hand via their cronies.

She thought Trudy might know some of the names, and felt it best to speak with her in person as well.

Esme visited the restaurant after school, in the lull between lunch and dinner, and found her seated at the end of the bar doing paperwork.

"Hi...!" Trudy greeted her by holding the "i" so long it started to sound like an "ee". She hugged Esme and the exertion made her run out of breath, unable to hold the note any longer.

This was the reception Esme had hoped for.

"What are you doing here?" Trudy asked. "Can I get you a glass of water? A soda?"

"No, thank you."

"It's from the gun," she reached over the bar to unhook the dispenser and hold it up. "Extra syrupy."

"I'm good," Esme held up her hand.

"Have a seat."

Esme took her up on that and sat next to her.

"I have a favor to ask," she said as she settled in. "And I hope it's not too forward."

"Really?" Trudy oversold her intrigue.

"It looks like we're doing a whole series on the local hospitality industry..."

"Right on," Trudy hung her hand up for a high-five.

Esme obliged before continuing.

"...and I want to pursue the same angle from last month, about whether the high-end has advantages over the standard, but from the ownership perspective."

"It doesn't matter to them how much money they put in, as long as they get more out."

"Maybe so. I'm already in the process of interviewing people in charge of the new hotel being built, and was hoping maybe I could get the names of the investors in this one."

"Sure," Trudy shrugged.

"I was going to check city hall, but it felt kind of devious, like I was sneaking around, when meanwhile I know people."

"You know people," she teased.

"People like you," Esme teased back.

"Aw…" Trudy slipped into some humility. "Well, I may not know all the names, but I know a bunch."

"The more, the better," Esme encouraged her. "Some of them won't agree to talk. A lot of rich people like to keep to themselves."

Trudy peeled off a piece of paper from the pad next to her work pile.

"You might recognize some of these names," she said as she jotted them down. "There's a few locals in the mix. Most of the heavy hitters are from out of town, only come in on special weekends."

It wasn't taking Trudy long to write the names, and Esme didn't take long to feel restless. While Trudy scribbled the latest name she could recall, Esme briefly wondered whether she should ask the question she ended up asking.

"Do other departments in the hotel have the same problem as you?"

"Which problem is that?" she asked back while keeping the names coming.

"Finding qualified workers?"

"They do," Trudy nodded as she wrote.

"Has anyone tried an employment agency or anything like that?"

"I don't know," she took a moment to consider the next name more than Esme's question. "I could see someone in maintenance or housekeeping maybe doing that."

"That reminds me," Esme reached the turn she had been signaling toward. "I've been meaning to talk to housekeeping."

"Dorothy?" Trudy returned to her list.

Esme jumped a little inside but tried to keep it low.

"What about her?"

"Do you want to follow up with her?"

"That's part of it, yes."

"How sweet," Trudy commented as she added another investor.

Esme let her do so in peace for a name or two.

"Does housekeeping have a manager who does the hiring?"

"They do," Trudy finished writing the current name with a flourish, indicating it was probably the last. "Her name is Paulina Munoz. Shall I introduce you?"

She handed over the list.

"No," Esme took the paper from her. "Thank you. For the offer and the names. I'll ask at the front desk. You're busy."

"Darn," Trudy grinned. "I was looking for an excuse to get away from inventory for a while."

"Sorry," Esme stood up.

"That's okay," Trudy joined her. "Thanks for keeping me honest."

"Thanks again for this," Esme waggled the paper before folding it and putting it in her pocket.

"Good to see you again," Trudy gave her another hug.

"I wish I was old enough for a girls' night out with you."

Trudy laughed and said, "In time."

Esme found out at the front desk that the housekeeping manager could see her in about ten minutes.

She sank into a plush love seat in the lobby and let it swallow her for a minute before biding her time by reading the list.

Rafa's father was one of them. A couple other names sounded familiar. One woman had an academic award named after her that Esme won in fifth grade for writing an essay on personal responsibility. It included a one hundred dollar cash prize. Her biggest purchase with the money was the boxed set of Percy Jackson books that now hid the evidence.

Paulina emerged and introduced herself as Mrs. Munoz.

Esme thought perhaps she would lead her back to her office, but Mrs. Munoz stood her ground in the lobby and asked what she could do for her.

"If I wanted to apply for a housekeeping job, would I turn in an application directly to you?"

"Yes."

"I was just wondering, because a friend of mine heard you go through an agency."

"We do both," she said. "It's seasonal work, and our number of applicants don't always line up with the seasons."

"If I put in an application with the agency, would that get my name out to all the other hotels, too?"

"It's not that kind of agency."

"What do you mean?"

Mrs. Munoz held an agitated pause.

"They're more like a contractor," she explained. "The workers are from other countries."

"Really?"

"On visas. Perfectly legal."

"Still..."

Esme kept her in suspense.

"What?" Mrs. Munoz asked that she not.

"That doesn't seem fair."

"To who?"

"Well, nobody."

Mrs. Munoz leaned back without actually leaning back.

"How so?" she asked at the peak of her illusion.

"I mean, is it really because of the seasons, or because you can pay them less?"

"Do you really want a job? Or are you already working for someone?"

"I don't get it," Esme played innocent.

Mrs. Munoz reviewed her performance.

"If it was up to me," she reached a verdict. "I wouldn't use them. But it's not my call."

Esme was fascinated.

"Then whose is it?"

"Our Human Resources director."

Esme nodded and considered asking for an appointment with the director, but thought that would be too revealing.

"I'm sorry if I came across as accusing you of anything," she said instead. "I was surprised to hear how that agency works."

Mrs. Munoz, meanwhile, considered unburdening herself some more, and unlike Esme, followed through.

"It's not only about the seasons," she said. "In fact, I'm not sure it has anything to do with that."

Esme tilted her head, and Mrs. Munoz took her cue.

"When you offer hard, unrewarding jobs with low wages, you risk blowing through the local workforce eventually. HR seems to think that's the case with us."

"And you don't agree?"

"We're competing with field labor, working the vineyards or orchards. Our jobs can look like paradise if we market them right."

"But they don't want to?"

"They don't have to."

"Why are you telling me this?" it occurred to Esme.

"Sorry."

"Don't be. I'm flattered."

"You're the first chance I've had to unload. I don't dare confront my boss. She's responsible for it. And my family hates when I talk about work."

Esme thought of the paper in her pocket.

"I wonder if the owners know about this."

"What makes you say that?" Mrs. Munoz asked.

"One of them has a son I go to school with. I was going to drop his name to help get the job."

Mrs. Munoz smiled.

"I wonder."

"I won't drop your name if I find myself talking about this again," Esme promised.

"Thank you."

"Thank you, Mrs. Munoz," Esme offered her hand.

"Paulina," she corrected her and accepted her offer.

Esme decided the smart move on ownership would be to work from the outside in, starting with the weekenders, and leaving the locals alone for as long as she could. She sat in her car in the resort parking lot and composed a list of the out-of-towners before visiting her contact at the airport who had been her main source on the "Who's Landing Here" story.

Jackson was a fifth-generation resident of the area who proudly stuck around after he graduated when Esme was a freshman. He was the kind of amiable soul who seemed destined to be content in life no matter what he did, the kind of soul Esme wanted to pity but probably envied.

He was a hundred yards out on the tarmac refueling an old Cal Fire air tanker when she arrived. She waved at him from the patio of the ten-table Landing Gear Diner that was only open for breakfast and lunch. He waved back and held up his index finger to let her know he'd be there once he was done keeping the nozzle in place.

Within minutes, he unhooked it and coiled the hose back around the rack of the fuel truck before driving toward the terminal.

"Is there a fire somewhere?" she asked as he stopped and idled next to her.

"Nah," he leaned out the window. "Just exercises."

"Thank God. That plane looks a little old to be coming to the rescue."

"Is this a long conversation? I gotta get the truck back to the hangar."

"I don't think so," she took out a copy of her list and handed it to him. "Do you know any of these people? I've been told some of them fly in here now and then."

"I do," he studied the lineup. "Hardly a weekend goes by without at least one of them passing through."

He tried handing it back to her.

"Keep it," she said. "Could you let me know next time one of them does?"

"Will do. Might have a bunch of them this weekend for the Grenache Festival."

"There's a Grenache Festival?"

"Yup."

"How long have we had that?"

"Don't know," Jackson shrugged. "Guess all the glamour grapes are spoken for."

"Can't wait for the Cab Franc Festival," Esme cracked.

Jackson chuckled.

"And if it's not too much to ask," Esme refocused. "Could you maybe try and get a sense of where they might be hanging out? 'Hey, sir, welcome back. Whaddya got planned for this weekend?' That sort of thing."

"Sure."

"I don't want to get you in trouble."

The air tanker started its engine.

"Me?" he shouted over the hum of the propellers. "Trouble?"

"Always a first time!" she matched his volume as the plane taxied away. "Thanks, Jackson!"

"Thank you, Ace! You make my job more interesting!"

He sent her updates on the investors' activities as each one arrived during an otherwise normal week for Esme, normal relative to the days since she received her first letter from Dorothy. The breather allowed her to speculate aloud over how her job as a professional student had become more interesting as well, since its relationship to the real world was more apparent thanks to her pursuit of justice.

"Is that what you're calling this?" Irma asked. "The pursuit of justice?"

"What would you call it?" Esme fired back. "And don't say padding my college application."

"Okay," Irma said.

Then she didn't say anything else.

"Dick," Esme muttered.

They were about to reach the intersection of the Science Building and the Humanities Center, where they would split up to reach their fifth period classes. If there was a part that bugged Esme about her most recent defense of the Dorothy effect, how it brought the real world and school closer together, it was the notion of a "real world" as opposed to the one she and her friends inhabited, as if meeting deadlines, keeping an exhausting schedule, and being held to vindictive standards wasn't a harsh reality.

As the junction in their path drew near, the latest text from Jackson landed in Esme's phone.

"What about this one?" Esme asked as she read his update. "The clambake at Oak Peak Winery."

"The clambake part sounds familiar."

"How many clambakes could there be?"

"Tanner has two events he's catering. If you can't work the clambake, I can double-check those other ones Jackson sent."

"I don't want to work it," Esme said. "I'll be pestering a resort owner. I can't be a server when I do that. Tanner will get in trouble."

They stopped at the crossroads of lunch and fifth period.

"You want me to work it and let you in," Irma supposed.

"That's right."

"So you want me to get in trouble."

"Nobody will know. Oak Peak is one of those huge wineries with all kinds of service doors."

"You'd better have a solid backstory for how you scored an invitation," Irma warned.

"If anybody asks," Esme doubted.

"Our friendship may depend on it," Irma said as she went her way.

Esme blew her a kiss before she went hers.

# CHAPTER 6

Esme was hoping someone would ask how she made her way into the clambake, eager as she was to perform the story she concocted. It was inspired by plenty of truth, based on her work for the school paper, but involved a fake article she was pretending to write about the Grenache Festival, titled "Why Grenache?"

For the sake of plausibility, she considered interviewing some other attendees before targeting her mark, whose name was Mark, but thought better of it in the event she was booted from the grounds before she could reach him.

She had researched Mark beforehand with the help of a tad more information from Jackson. His father was a San Diego surgeon who had turned a few tweaks to some medical devices into millions of dollars and who died young from the stress that came with the windfall, which led to Mark's career as the sole inheritor of the fortune.

Esme had no trouble identifying him, as a photo opportunity and press release appeared to come standard with any of his investments. There was Mark at the UCSD Medical Center clutching the middle third of a big cardboard check along with two other donors, and there he was posing on the first tee at Torrey Pines with a PGA tour pro during a charity event, and there he was shaking hands with the backup catcher of the San Diego Padres to herald a donation to the team's inner city youth baseball program.

And here was Mark at the Grenache Festival clambake, temporarily abandoned by his date at one of the temporary outdoor bars composed of a wooden plank resting on two wine barrels.

"Hi," she seized the opportunity and rested her elbows on the bar next to him.

"Hello," he raised his eyebrows along with his glass of red as if to hide behind it.

"Grenache?" she nodded at the wine he was quaffing.

"Zin," he answered with a gulp.

"They should have a festival for that."

Mark didn't respond. He had guzzled too large a dose and was wrestling with the aftermath.

"I know I'm a little young for a wine event," Esme acknowledged.

"Okay," he came up for air and tried to catch up with what was happening.

"I'm working on a story for my high school paper about the Grenache Festival. Can I get a quote from you?"

"Absolutely," he relaxed at the prospect of more exposure.

"Thank you," she enthused as she produced her phone. "First, can I get your name?"

"Mark Drogitis."

She tapped it onto her keypad.

"And where are you from?"

"San Diego."

"Cool," she kept tapping. "What do you do down there?"

"Venture capitalist."

"Nice. So do you have any business interests up here? Or is this strictly pleasure?"

"It's pleasure, but I do have some investments."

"Ooh..."

"I'm a partner at Snell Winery and the Tuscan resort."

Esme paused for effect before continuing to record his answers.

"What?" he asked.

"Huh?"

"You hesitated."

"I did? Sorry."

"Why?"

She pretended to almost say something and catch herself.

"What?" Mark encouraged her.

"It's probably nothing."

Mark's date returned and occupied the space between them. She was close to age-appropriate, and slid her arm under his upon registering the intensity between him and a teenage girl.

"What's going on?" she asked.

"This young woman may have some information about Snell Winery I should know about."

"You're local?" his date asked.

"Yes," Esme detected some arrogance in the question.

"Lucky," she softened up. "I love it here."

"The winery," Mark pressed the issue. "What's the deal?"

Esme exhaled.

"It's not the winery," she admitted. "It's the resort."

"Yes...?" he elongated the word.

"A friend of mine works there," she launched her story. "And one of the housekeepers told her that she and some of the others are part of a human trafficking ring."

"Oh my God," his date exclaimed before she turned to Mark. "Did she just come up to you to tell you this?"

"No," Esme explained. "I'm writing an article for my school paper about the Grenache Festival and it came up."

"How does it work?" she took over the conversation.

"The trafficking?" Esme asked.

"Yes. What do they do to them?"

Mark jumped back in.

"We don't know if it's true," he reminded them.

His date ignored him.

"Do they have to do anything?" she asked. "You know, besides clean the rooms? Do they even clean the rooms?"

"They clean the rooms," Esme assured her. "It's nothing like that. As far as she knows. An agency tricks them into coming over from the Philippines, saying it's well-paid work with a nice place to stay, but then they shove them all in a seedy motel room and take most of their money to pay off some debts they make up as they go along."

"That sucks," the date quacked.

"So they're here legally," Mark wanted to know.

"Yes."

"Alright, then," he was relieved.

Both Esme and the date glared at him.

"Well," he prepared his defense. "They're getting paid, so it's not like it's slavery, and they're not being forced into prostitution."

The two women waited for more.

"That's it?" the date asked when nothing else arrived.

"They're not here illegally," he rephrased his earlier point.

The date groaned, shook her head, drained her glass, and left the bar.

Mark looked at Esme for some sympathy, which she did not provide. He scowled at her before chasing after his date, weaving through the woozy crowd.

Esme watched the pursuit and tried not to smile in case he looked back. When the chase led them into the visitor center, she turned back to the bar and would have ordered a glass of wine if she was old enough, but could only fist-pump.

Blake executed a double fist-pump the next day at the resort when Esme tracked him down at the valet parking station to tell him he was right about the letters, that they were between her and one of the housekeepers who was, in fact, named Dorothy.

"I knew it," he followed up his pump action by coming out from behind the podium and flinging his arm downward as though spiking a football in the driveway.

Esme wasn't concerned with anyone eavesdropping, as she had waited to approach him during a lull in the flow of cars.

"It gets better," she tempted him. "I need you to be my eyes and ears here at the resort."

He raised his arms and walked slowly towards her.

She proceeded with the details of her request before he had a chance to hug her.

"There may be some tension between the HR director and the housekeeping manager," she said. "Also, some of the owners may come in on edge and have some intense conversations with management. Let me know when that happens. Describe it as best you can, take pictures or videos if possible."

"Is Trudy on our team, too?" he hoped.

"We need to keep her out of this," she said, which made Blake feel more proud than disappointed.

"You think she may be in on it?" he probed. "Not sure who to trust?"

"No," she popped his bubble. "This is her career. I don't want to jeopardize it. You park cars."

"True," he agreed as though they were talking about someone else.

"That's one of your best features, Blake. You're impossible to insult."

"What exactly is going on here?" he had already moved on. "The letters made it sound bad, but they were like starting to watch a movie from the middle."

She caught him up on the basics of the scam and the moves she had made so far, pausing twice to let him greet guests and park their vehicles.

"What motel did you say they're keeping them in?" he asked as he jogged back from the reserved spaces for the second time.

"I didn't."

"Well then," he caught his breath. "What motel are they keeping them in?"

"I'm not telling you."

"Come on..."

"No."

"What do you think I'll do?"

"Something stupid."

"I can be insulted, Esme. I can reach a point."

"Look," she leveled with him. "I said I don't want to jeopardize Trudy's career. But I also don't want to put you in any danger. Please…"

Blake sulked.

"I don't know what these people are capable of," she continued her plea. "Everything is in the shadows. They could be really violent. Dorothy certainly thinks so. She's very frightened. Think of her. You might be able to take care of yourself, but don't put those women in harm's way."

"All right," he relented.

"Thank you."

"But can I stare down the van when it pulls in?" he grinned.

"Sure," she granted.

"I'll come around the front and be all…" he threw open his arms, "What's up?"

"Blake…"

"I'm kidding," he assured her. "How stupid do you think I am?"

He smiled at her, daring her to say something.

She refused, smiling back instead.

Enlisting Blake for surveillance was like directing a show. She spent the week feeding him lines and cues while he was on the job. The texts scrolling between them looked like a storyboard outline. She told him to casually mention to the HR Director that it seemed as though some of the owners were stopping by more often than usual, and to report on her reaction. ("She said yes, they were, and she was all pissed about it.") She told him to express concern over her reaction next time he had the chance, and to ask if something was wrong. ("She said they want things done no questions asked so they can take credit and not take any responsibility.")

By the end of the week a picture was emerging of trouble in paradise, and she was proud to be painting it.

She also took pride in drafting Blake, for seeing value in someone she had always dismissed as an idiot. She counted it as evidence of her growth and maturation.

She expected to compile more evidence in support of her maturity when she updated Daisy on the status of her investigation during their latest date with Irma at the taqueria.

The afternoon started out pleasantly enough.

Irma was convinced their AP History teacher was in the habit of saying "supposably", with a "b", instead of "supposedly", but it was hard to tell since he used the word as verbal filler, with the frequency some people use the word "literally" or "right?", so it would fly by quickly. Daisy and Esme had never noticed, but were intrigued, and tried to come up with a diplomatic way to ask him to repeat it, or a cunning way to lure him into using it in a sentence.

When they failed to map out a promising plan, Esme took advantage of the impasse to share what she thought of as a successful operation.

For five minutes, she didn't take a bite of her burrito as she re-enacted highlights from the conversations she had baited people into having with her over the past week, both in person and through Blake. At the conclusion of her summary, she took a bite that tasted especially delicious. It was the same old burrito, but now seemed to be accompanied by applause.

Irma appeared ready to offer some of the cheers Esme was imagining.

But Daisy didn't play her part.

"Are you kidding?" she asked instead. "You're not conducting an investigation. You're creating chaos."

Irma laughed until she realized she should not, which only took a second.

"What do you mean?" Esme demanded of Daisy.

"Oh my God, where do I start," Daisy prepared to ignore her food for the time being. "You're not presenting yourself as a reporter. You're pretending to talk to people for other reasons, so everything is off the record. And when you do tell people you're working on a story for the paper, you misrepresent what you're writing about. We can't use any of it. This is our school paper, not a sting operation."

"I'm forcing people to face facts."

"I thought you finished the Journalism Literacy Module," Daisy ignored her defense.

"Those online quiz thingies?"

"Yes," Daisy grew more suspicious.

"Yes," Esme echoed. "I did them."

"Really?"

"Well..."

"I knew it."

"I got a lot of help from Lindsey."

"As in she pretty much gave you the answers."

"I wouldn't say 'pretty much.'"

"Okay. Gave you the answers."

"I was going to say 'sort of.'"

"Those 'quiz thingies' cover everything you need to know about ethics and standards."

"Ethics and standards shouldn't be shoved into some online module," Esme tried to broaden the subject, if not change it. "They're far too important."

Daisy glared.

Irma intervened.

"I think it's nice that Esme is being honest," she said.

Her contention only aroused more suspicion in Daisy.

"Have you really called ICE?" she asked Esme.

Esme had lied to her before about calling, so it wasn't that hard to lie again.

"Yes," she said.

Daisy was skeptical.

Esme understood and buried her understanding with words.

"They should bust them any day now," she dug in. "It's a big agency. They have a lot on their plate."

Daisy turned her attention toward her own plate that held the last half of her chile relleno. She lowered her head in a mournful manner, as though she was about to finish more than her food.

"And when they do bust them," Esme continued, "that's it for me. No more chasing the story. No more chaos. You don't have to pull me off the piece. ICE will do it for you."

"Ice, ice, baby," Irma rapped in a desperate attempt to ease the tension.

Daisy ignored her and focused on Esme despite looking down at her plate.

"It's not only unethical," she picked up a fork and toyed with taking a bite. "It's immoral."

"I'm getting results," Esme joined Irma in trying to lighten the mood. "So it may not be smack dab in the middle of moral city, but it's moral adjacent."

"Stop acting," Daisy kept her eyes lowered.

"Excuse me?" Esme heard her, but asked anyway.

"Stop acting," Daisy looked up. "Everything is a performance with you. You're not even a good student. You're performing the part of one."

"Daisy…" Irma cautioned her.

"And you don't play your part?" Esme straightened up.

"Esme…" Irma cautioned her.

"No," Daisy was the first to raise her voice, if only slightly. "This matters to me."

"You don't play along with Mr. Hawley when you think he's full of shit?" Esme matched her tone. "You don't think half the staff are idiots, and wish you could tell them they are?"

"That's decency," Daisy settled down into her previous range. "That's manners."

"Where are those things now?" Esme wasn't ready to join her back in a lower register.

"Sometimes people don't deserve them."

"You don't like what I'm doing for your precious paper, so you trash my entire character," Esme was near tears, fidgeting as though considering a sudden exit.

Irma looked at Daisy as if to say Esme had a point, but Daisy was already relenting.

"I'm sorry, Esme," she said. "I was wrong."

"No, you're not."

"I am. I'm very sorry. I went too far."

"No," Esme wiped her eyes with a napkin and settled down. "I mean, you're not wrong. I'm way out of line."

"I'm the one who's out of line," Daisy reached for her hand.

Esme let her have it but could not look at her.

"I needed to hear those things," she confessed. "I'm an ambitious cliché, that character who makes all the money in the world but loses her family and friends."

"I wouldn't go that far," Daisy held on to a straight face. "But you're right about me. I have no room to talk. I'm no less ambitious than you are, but I hide behind being the editor of the paper, like it's way more than a high school activity, like it's some noble cause."

"You know," Irma leaned in as if setting up a concession of her own. "I'm sure glad I'm not like you guys."

Daisy laughed a little louder than Esme, who was still in recovery. She absorbed the punch line with a series of nods that seemed to transform the tears on her face from sadness to joy, or at least relief.

"Thanks for calling me out," she said as the reactions dimmed. "I'm pretty certain I wanted to do the right thing, and I thought my shallowness would help. I could perform for a good cause. But...."

She tossed her hands in the air and let them fall.

"There's still time to do it right," Daisy assured her.

Esme stuck out her lower lip, blew air up across her cheeks to dry them, and agreed.

They finished their food while pondering if it mattered whether someone said "supposably" instead of "supposedly", and alerting one another in silence to the elderly couple at the next table who were either aghast at the argument they had witnessed between Daisy and Esme, or anticipating another one.

Their relentless gaping eventually overwhelmed anything else the girls could think to discuss. They surrendered any further conversation and started a contest to see who could best imitate the neighboring couple.

Irma tapped out first, and leaned into the other table.

"It's a thin line," she said to the aged pair.

Rather than reacting with embarrassment or offense, they were pleasantly surprised to be noticed.

"So true," the wife said to the appreciative chuckle of her husband.

Esme and Irma were quiet on their way back to campus for Esme's rehearsal and Irma's International Club meeting. They needed rest after the unexpected intensity of their date with Daisy. Everyone may have left on good terms, but that couldn't erase what had been said before the treaty.

Irma asked Esme a question while they waited at the last light before the parking lot.

"Have you really called Zack?"

Esme exhaled.

Irma did too.

"I'm going to," Esme got the car rolling again as the light changed.

"The sooner you do, the less you lied to Daisy."

"That's how I see it."

She pulled into a parking spot.

They both saw Gina Ruiz from behind, walking through the front gate. Irma leaned back in the seat and appeared to brace herself.

"Is she in International Club now?" Esme asked.

"Yes," Irma groaned.

"I'm surprised she doesn't bring the Afghan girl with her."

"She usually does. Mariam has tutoring before the meeting, so she's a little late sometimes."

"Mariam? That's her name?"

"She's very sweet."

"That's nice."

They sat and watched Gina walk out of sight.

Esme didn't hate her. She didn't know her.

They went to different middle schools and first got wind of one another during the winter concerts, when the bands from the two schools combined forces for a show at the high school auditorium. Gina's friends would tell her Esme was the Gina of their school, and Esme's friends would tell her Gina was the Esme of their school. They stole glances at each other, never saying hello. They ended up in a lot of classes together in high school, since they were on the same track, and were cordial when on the same team in a group project. But they remained at a distance, adhering to an unspoken agreement, like a family who won't acknowledge their daughter's prison sentence or their son's boyfriend.

"Mariam is in a safe place," Irma said. "Dorothy is not."

"I know."

"And it's not like Gina is helping her. She still has to go back to Afghanistan at the end of the semester. You're doing something better."

Assuming she did it.

Irma opened the door. Instead of saying goodbye before she left, she said "Call Zack."

Esme intended to call him after rehearsal, but it was Friday, and she changed her mind because she figured they probably weren't as well-staffed on the weekends, so she vowed to call Monday morning.

Someone called her after rehearsal, though.

"Rafa?" she confirmed the name on her screen.

"I know," he said. "I promised an evite for a party coming up. And here I am calling. But we've got a few friends on their way over, sort of a spur-of-the-moment thing, and I was hoping to hang out with you before the next big, loud thing."

"I just got out of rehearsal," Esme bought some time as she caught up with what was happening. "I'm a bit of a mess."

"Come over whenever you can make it."

"Can I bring a plus-one?"

"Eh..."

"No?"

"Trying to keep this small."

"Fair enough."

"I'll send you the location."

"Okay," she had yet to commit.

"See you then."

He ended the call as she continued to consider his offer.

She wasn't really a mess. Her section of the ensemble had spent the whole two hours standing around the piano rehearsing their songs, trying to harmonize, so she didn't need to freshen up or change.

A map popped onto her screen with a pin marking Rafa's address. She already had a general idea where it was. They lived in the hills, as the wealthy often do, but she had never driven through their neighborhood, much less past their house.

She tapped on the street view of the map to see a photo of the block. Their house was not visible. It stood somewhere behind a gate and a hedge two stories high. Going there at night would make it even more mysterious and majestic. Such a reveal was too tempting to pass up.

She stopped for coffee on the way to fill the time she pretended to need.

When she arrived at the entrance, she texted Rafa for the code. He sent it with an apology for not relaying it earlier.

"It's been a while since anyone new has come through the gate."

Esme thought this curious, considering how gregarious he was around campus.

The house was made of sections, many of them on stilts, as if being on a hill was still not high enough. These elevated rooms were made of glass and filled with light, looking more like museum displays or showroom floors than offices or bedrooms. That nobody appeared to be inside any of them only added to the effect. Every tree on the front grounds had a light planted at its base, pointing up the trunk and into its leaves. Every shrub concealed a light inside of it aimed at a footpath or at the stairs leading up to the front door. Esme would have been suspicious if there had not been plenty of cars in the driveway.

She supposed there was a chance they all belonged to Rafa's family, but she heard a party-sized group of people through the door as she approached it. She doubted the doorbell could be heard above the din of conversation, but Rafa answered within seconds.

"Yes!" he came in for a hug. "I was afraid you'd changed your mind."

"I would have called."

"Texted."

"Yeah, who calls anymore?"

He acknowledged her taunt with an air tally mark, and beckoned her inside.

"We keep the parties down low," he narrated their passage into the living room. "On the ground floor and in the basement."

Esme noticed the guests looked older. She struggled to recognize anyone.

"Is this your party?" she asked. "Or your parents'?"

"Their friends are my friends," he said as they reached a kitchen with an island of alcohol in the center flanked by trays of tapas.

"Like Bruno here," he slapped a man on the shoulder who was hunched over one of the trays. Bruno turned with a start and recovered with a smile after he swallowed his current bite.

"Known him since I was up to his knee," Rafa continued. "Longer than anyone I went to school with. Why wouldn't we be friends?"

Bruno returned Rafa's shoulder slap with one of his own.

"How's it going, kiddo?"

"Swimmingly, my good man," Rafa made way for an introduction. "This is Esme, one of my friends who was born in this century."

"Pleased to meet you," Esme said.

"Likewise," Bruno swiped his hand on the back of his pants and held it out to shake hers.

"Bruno owns the lumber yard on Creekside, and...what else, Bruno? You've got so damn much real estate I've lost track."

"That's it," Bruno said. "I sold the gas stations."

"Congratulations?" Rafa framed it as a question.

"Yeah," Bruno assured him. "It's good news. I'm semi-retiring."

"From what?" Rafa teased, then rubbed Bruno's belly and jostled him before he could return fire. "You know I'm kidding."

Rafa and Esme moved on as Bruno put himself back together while Esme said it was nice meeting him.

"No, seriously," Rafa muttered as they made their way around the island. "Retire from what?"

Esme smiled and wondered what the rest of the people owned.

"Do you want anything?" Rafa gestured to the food and drink. "Caprese kabob? Lamb slider? Tanqueray and tonic?"

"I'm good."

"Let the record show I wasn't actually offering you liquor," he said while leading her out of the kitchen.

"I figured," she said in stride. "Oh, was I supposed to laugh when you did that?"

He grinned and wagged a finger at her.

They re-entered the living room at the far end and headed for a downward stairway.

"The basement," he announced.

"Is that where the people our age are hanging out?"

Rafa chuckled as they began their descent.

"Don't think of them as old rich people," he said. "Think of them as scholarship opportunities."

The basement looked as though it was designed for a younger crowd, with a video screen that nearly covered an entire wall, some throwback arcade games lining another wall, and a foosball table in the middle. But that younger crowd was not present. Rafa and Esme stood on the bottom step overlooking the balding and coiffed heads. All of them were standing, since the chairs and sofas were so low that even if they could get in them, they couldn't get out.

"What am I doing here?" Esme asked Rafa.

He appeared to have an answer that he was reluctant to share.

"Let me show you the wine cellar."

Which was the kind of thing she would expect him to say with a lot more aplomb than he did.

They weaved through the perfume and cologne and arrived at a door that looked as though it led to a closet or a bathroom, but when he opened it, a new dimension seemed to unfurl before them.

The room was longer and wider than the house, an extension of the basement that spread far beyond the boundaries above. It was well-lighted, but the glow was soft, like at an expensive restaurant with a sparse, modern design. Ten-foot tall racks of wine bottles reached far into what seemed to be a horizon rather than a wall. The bottles rested on their sides, the tops pointing into the aisles like gun barrels. The sight was so impressive that Esme didn't notice the man materializing from the next aisle into the one they stood in until Rafa introduced him.

"Esme, this is my father," he moderated. "Dad, this is Esme."

"A pleasure," Mr. Barajas shook her hand with a grip that was firm but not too self-conscious.

"This is really beautiful," Esme said. "And I don't even like wine. Not that I've tried it."

Mr. Barajas smiled.

"You didn't sneak a little bit when you were at the Grenache Festival interviewing Mark?"

She thought it best to remain silent.

"There's only one high school newspaper in town," he addressed how he knew. "And one student working there who fits your description. Will you excuse us, son?"

Rafa obliged and avoided eye contact with Esme on his way out.

The sound of the door shutting flapped up and down the rows of racks.

Mr. Barajas waited for the echo to fade before speaking.

"There's also one idiot on our executive board at the resort. That would be Mark. I would prefer you not quote him."

"My editor said we probably can't use his quotes, anyway."

"I can give you some."

"Okay..."

She reached for her phone to record him, but he produced a sheet of paper twice-folded from his back pocket and held it like a torch that lit a space between them.

"A response to your allegations," he proclaimed. "It says we on the executive board trust that our Human Resources Department has abided by state and federal law in our hiring practices, and we shall continue to put our faith in them unless our ongoing investigation of the matter compels us otherwise."

"Thanks for the hard copy," she took his statement and waved it in recognition before transferring it to her back pocket.

"Rafa says you're quite the scholar," he softened his tone, but his body language did not follow.

"I try."

"And you're a junior?"

"Yes."

"What schools are you applying to next year?"

"The usual, I guess you could say, for a West Coast Type A teenager."

Mr. Barajas delighted in her answer and further loosened up.

"I hope that includes the usual private schools," he said.

"It does."

"Sometimes you can get a better financial aid package from them. They work a little harder than the state schools to bring down their prices since their base tuition is so prohibitive for most families."

"That's what my counselor said."

"Of course, all that really does is make the projected costs of the public schools and the private schools come out about equal. The hot spot is that number between what a university defines as a family's financial need and their expected contribution. The net price. And that gap has dashed a lot of dreams. An acceptance letter is fun, but it's only page one."

"I've heard stories."

"It often falls upon merit scholarships to ease that burden."

"I'm applying for as many of those as I'm eligible for."

"This article about the resort could help," he said. "Your story has a lot of potential."

She didn't want to ask what exactly he meant by that, but it was all she could think of, so there was nothing left to say.

"It was nice meeting you, Mr. Barajas," she excused herself. "Your home is lovely."

"Thank you for your consideration," he called after her as she reached the door.

She turned to see if there was anything more to read in his expression, but he was facing the rack of bottles closest to him, running his fingers over their necks.

Rafa was anxiously waiting outside the door, as though the basement was a hospital lobby rather than a rec room. He may as well have asked if the operation was a success when he asked her how things went with his father.

"You and your smarmy theory," she dismissed him on her way to the stairs.

"What?" he followed her.

"Your bullshit about college being rigged for the rich," she started her climb.

"You don't think it is?" he kept up.

"Of course it is," she stopped at the top of the staircase on the edge of the living room. "And if you convince enough people to believe it's nothing but a scam, then fewer people will bother trying, and you can get things back to the way they used to be."

"Come on," he protested.

"Less competition for those already in power."

"Oh, please."

"It's refreshing in a way. Ditch the pretense. Just own up to reality." She headed for the front door.

"You want to talk about reality?" he followed her there, too.

"I'm not so sure," she elbowed her way through the local oligarchs. "I think I've had my share for the night."

He passed her and made it to the door first.

"You can change the world," he said.

"Thanks," she reached for the doorknob. "Inspiring, as always."

"I wasn't done," he put his hand over hers on the knob.

"Oh?" she jerked hers away and put both hands on her hips.

"You can change the world," he started over. "Or you can be a part of it. You can't have it both ways."

She held her power pose longer than anyone would expect before she spoke.

"Barf," she said.

Then she let herself out.

In her agitation, she wanted to drive fast down the hill, taking the curves like a stunt driver. But she was unfamiliar with the terrain, so she had to go slow and tap the brakes frequently, which made her even more frustrated and prone to yelling so loudly that she was light-headed and temporarily hoarse after each outburst.

# CHAPTER 7

By sunrise the next morning she was ready to kneecap the confidence expressed by Mr. Barajas on behalf of his breed on the board, but she had to wait until the world went to work.

"You at the resort today?" she texted Blake.

"I make bank on Saturdays," he texted back.

"So yes?"

"Already here."

"Is the HR Director there today?"

"Let me check."

Esme stared at her screen while she waited and felt as though she was driving down the winding road from Rafa's house again. Blake took about the same amount of time to reply as it took her to reach the bottom of the hill the night before.

"In the office at 10."

She murmured a curse at having to wait a few more hours, but at least the Director was going to be there. She thanked Blake and started writing a draft of the story to pass the time. With so many events left to unfold, and so much of her work so far unusable, there was very little content to play with. About all she could do was sketch a distant likeness of Dorothy's circumstances, and outline the kind of scam that very likely targeted her.

Before she left for the resort, she grabbed one of Dorothy's receipts from their hiding place in her book shelf. She was tempted to use it for quicker access to the Human Resources office, in dramatic fashion, by handing it to an unwitting concierge to give to the Director as an ominous calling card. But she kept it to herself so that the Director would not have time to prepare a defense, and in case she tried to play dumb.

Besides, it turned out Esme only had to wait a minute to see her.

She played by the rules and identified herself as a reporter.

The Director introduced herself as Megan, and cheerfully attempted to see if they could keep their conversation in the lobby.

"I loved the article you wrote in your paper last month," she said. "So sweet."

"Thank you."

"Are you writing a sequel or something?"

"You could say that."

"So what can I do for you?"

"Has Mr. Barajas, or any of the other owners, spoken with you recently about the employment agency you've contracted to hire some of your housekeepers?"

Her smile sank.

"Let's go to my office."

Her work space did not match the pizzazz of the public space. It could have been the manager's office at the Riverbed Motel. Her gray swivel chair looked like it had been found abandoned next to a dumpster, and her desk appeared to be made of leftover metal filing cabinets. Megan sat down behind it and offered Esme the chair in front. She refused, and not because the chair was yet another forlorn piece of furniture in need of disinfectant, but because she felt like standing would help her apply pressure even if her words didn't come out the way she hoped.

"What about the employment agency?" Megan asked.

"Most of your money is paying them, not your workers."

Esme pulled out the receipt and handed it to Megan, who either studied it carefully or simply stared at it while she thought of what to say next.

"We had no idea they were doing this sort of thing," she passed it back.

"Is that 'we' as in you and the owners?" Esme reminded her of the initial question. "Or is that sort of a royal 'we', like you're speaking for the whole resort?"

"Nobody in upper management or ownership has spoken with me about this. They're unaware, as far as I know."

"And you didn't suspect anything, either."

"Not a thing."

"So this is all the agency's fault."

Megan's head emphatically vibrated up and down.

Esme considered sharing the Barajas spin about where responsibility lied, but looked around the overcast office with its skid marks on the floor and spackle on the walls, and elected to leave her alone.

"Thank you for your time, Megan. Hopefully we can still get a sweet story out of this."

As she walked through the lobby, she wondered whom the employment agency would blame if she questioned them. It was a sarcastic thought, but as she folded Dorothy's bill to put it away, sincerity struck.

The company name at the top of the page had no phone number under it. As much as they didn't want their employees to contact them, they must have a way to communicate with their employers.

She took a step toward Megan's office but decided to try and seek the number on her own. Their contact information was the first hit listed after she searched the name on her phone, which she didn't use to call them. Daisy wouldn't like it, but Esme didn't want her number or name to pop up in the agency's network, whether it was an office or a person with a cell phone.

"Hey, Blake," she caught him at the valet station between sprints to the parking lot. "Is there a house phone I can use?"

"Right here," he gestured to a phone on the desk below the key rack.

"Dial nine for an outside line?" she asked while lifting the receiver.

"Yup," he confirmed. "Who you calling, sneaky?"

"You'll see."

She finished dialing and caught a glimpse of the resort logo on Blake's windbreaker.

"How do you pronounce the name of this place?" she asked him while she waited for someone to pick up.

"I still don't know," he admitted.

A woman answered. Esme chose a pronunciation and sold it with poise.

"I'm from Human Resources," she further developed her character, "and I'm calling about the housekeepers you sent us recently."

"Yes?" the woman said as though she had already fielded a hundred other calls that morning.

"We have reason to believe your company is withholding way more money from their paychecks than necessary."

"How do you know what's necessary?"

"Excuse me?"

"We have expenses. We got them the job."

Esme held the phone away and stared at it. Blake laughed and she shushed him before putting it back to her ear.

"I know pretty much their whole check is gone by the time you give it to them," she threw herself deeper into her role. "That seems unnecessary."

"Talk to the foreman," the woman sighed.

"The foreman?"

"The guy who takes care of them, drives the van and shit. That guy."

"There's two of them."

"The other guy must be his friend. We only use one for each job. Standard practice."

"Is that how you keep your prices so low?" Esme sank to her level.

"Talk to the foreman," she said again before hanging up.

Esme stood in awe after putting the phone down.

"What?" Blake asked.

She started to speak twice, looked back at the resort, then into the distance before succeeding the third time, but only to a degree.

"I can't..."

"That bad?"

"The worst."

"Maybe you caught someone on a bad day."

Esme shook her head and waved her arms.

"Maybe you caught their worst employee," Blake tried again.

She bought into that a bit more.

"Still," she wondered, "if the rest are even one-tenth as revolting as that thing I just talked to, then why?"

She gestured about the resort grounds before letting her hands fall by her side.

"Why run a beautiful place like this and do business with that scum?" she gave voice to her motions.

Blake had an answer ready.

"Because it's busy and they're cheap."

Esme appreciated the simplicity, but saw something more.

"And responsible."

"They're scum but they're responsible?" Blake puzzled.

"Not responsible like mature or trustworthy," she explained. "They can take the blame."

"For what?"

"For whatever crappy things you would do if you didn't have to worry about your image."

Blake processed what she said. He looked down the driveway as if looking for a vehicle to park, for money that would pass directly between him and the customer rather than through the resort.

Esme was about to say goodbye and thank him when he added to the discussion.

"I wonder if that housekeeping agency has someone they point their finger at."

Which gave Esme an idea.

"They do."

On the way to her car, she called Irma and asked if she'd join her on a trip to The Riverbed to visit the foreman and his friend.

"Sounds like a job for Blake," Irma said. "Or a bunch of dudes like Blake."

"We're not busting the maids out," Esme clarified. "They won't even be there. They're at work. I just want to talk to the foremen, and I need your Spanish."

"My Spanish is half-assed. Ask my grandma."

"Between mine and yours, we'll be a complete ass."

"You said those guys guarding them are scary."

"That was then," Esme reached her car and slid into the driver's seat. "Now I've learned it's amateur hour up there. Plus it was dark last time. I didn't even see them that well. I'm pretty sure they're just a couple of guys trying to make rent."

"Pretty sure?"

"Pretty positive."

"Have you called Zack?"

"I've also learned that nobody will face any consequences unless I get this story right."

"You haven't called Zack."

"As soon as his team goes in, everybody gets to wash their hands of the whole thing. Just watch. But I'll have a surprise for them."

"Thank God for you."

"So you're not coming with me?"

"I didn't say that."

Esme smiled and looked up at the ceiling of her car as though she could see right through it to the sky.

"I'll see you in five minutes," she beamed.

"Roger," Irma said. "Or should I say 'Affirmative'?"

"Either one."

"Over and out?"

Esme hung up and started the car.

The town surrounding The Riverbed looked more sad than scary in the daylight.

"Were you ever afraid of the dark?" Esme asked Irma as they drove slowly over the lumpy road through the defeated homes.

"Every kid is at some point," Irma said.

"I'm thinking of what my Mom used to tell me, how there's nothing in the dark that isn't there in the light."

"Mine said that, too."

"But there's some really depressing things in the light you can't see in the dark."

"Don't be afraid of the dark, honey," Irma imitated a mother. "Be depressed about the light."

"Thanks, Mom."

Esme nearly parked across the street from The Riverbed before remembering the last time she staked out the place and that angry person who was most likely a woman banged on her window. This wasn't a stakeout, anyway, so she parked right in front of the old motel, hoping the action symbolized the boldness they needed to follow through on her idea.

They looked through the windshield down the narrow courtyard that split the bungalows. The van was not there, but two men were seated on the stoop in front of a unit Esme assumed was the one where the housekeepers were stored. One of the men was large, the other small. They turned their heads toward Esme and Irma. Their eyes were not visible in the shadows cast by the brims of their mesh baseball caps branded with the logos of ag companies, but they were obviously staring at the girls.

Esme took a deep breath.

"Let's go."

They got out and shut their doors at the same time, which prompted a look between them that lightened their mood and boosted their confidence. Something about the smaller man sneezing as the girls approached also helped make the situation less intimidating, and the fact both men stood up to greet them rather than stay seated.

"Hello," they all said to one another in Spanish, then introduced themselves.

The large, burly man called himself Oso. The small, spindly one was Edwin.

Irma said that she and Esme were working on a school project about local workers from other countries, and when they heard about the housekeepers from the Philippines, thought their project might stand out if they included some people from a country besides Mexico.

"So of course you interview a couple of Mexicans," Edwin said.

Laughter started slowly but spread as everyone realized it was okay to laugh.

Edwin sneezed again. Irma blessed him. He thanked her.

Esme's first question was easy to translate, so she managed it on her own.

"Where is the van?" she asked.

"Don't know," said Oso. "It belongs to our boss."

"Your boss?" Esme pried.

"Yes," he thought nothing of sharing. "Frankie."

The next question she wanted to ask made her nervous, so she turned to Irma.

"Ask them if Frankie is the one who usually picks up the women at the hotel."

She did, and Oso said "He always picks them up."

Esme pulled the receipt from her pocket and handed it to Edwin.

"Do you give this to the women?" she asked.

Edwin held up the bill and the two of them looked it over as if it was posted on a bulletin board.

Edwin sneezed and apologized, blaming it on his allergies. He handed the receipt to Oso, who answered the question.

"We hand them envelopes sometimes. Is this what's in them?"

"Yes."

Oso and Edwin looked at each other in shame.

"We're just paid to protect them," Oso said in their defense as he handed back the bill.

Esme and Irma exchanged a compassionate glance over the word 'protect' before Esme relied on Irma for the next question.

"How do you get paid?"

"Cash," Oso said, as Edwin was too busy nursing his runny eyes and nose with a bandana he brandished from his pocket.

"Frankie pays you?" Esme jumped back in.

"Yes," he answered.

Esme took a moment with Irma.

"Frankie must be the foreman the agency was talking about," she told her. "These guys are one more shield, another way for everyone to keep their distance."

Irma took that as a cue.

"How did you get this job?" she asked them.

"At the farm supply," Oso said. "It's one of the places where Frankie parks. We went to see what he had. This job was too long and the pay was too low for the other guys. Edwin took it to get out of the fields because of his allergies."

"Frankie thought I was too small," Edwin added. "He wanted me to have some backup."

"So I thought it over," Oso said. "And I realized it's like taking a break but getting paid a little for it."

Edwin sneezed. Irma blessed him again, but he said not to bother anymore.

"You'll lose your voice," he joked.

They all laughed without hesitation, and Esme thanked them for their time.

"Is Frankie at the farm supply?" Irma asked.

"Oh, yeah," Esme said. "I should have thought of that."

"Probably," Edwin said before preparing for a sneeze that never quite arrived.

"Congratulations," Esme held up her arm as if toasting him, and everyone shared a final moment of warmth before they left.

Neither Esme nor Irma spoke until they were on the freeway.

"Now I'm conflicted," Irma said.

"Me, too," Esme agreed.

"I hope they don't go to jail."

"Can we talk to Zack?"

"What would we tell him?"

"To leave them alone when things go down."

"Maybe we can talk to Edwin and Oso instead," Irma said. "Warn them when you call, tell them to get out of there."

"Or maybe not call."

Irma appeared to agree before correcting herself.

"I know," Esme also caught herself. "Nice guys, but Dorothy."

"If we just let it play out, who knows how long the ladies are stuck there."

"And Edwin and Oso might be replaced with some real bad asses who treat them like crap."

"Edwin and Oso," Irma said their names like they were puppies.

"I know," Esme made a pouty face.

"Dammit!" Irma yelled.

"Why did you have to be so adorable, Edwin and Oso!"

"What if you call, or break the story, whatever you have to do to get into Stanford, but then we take them to prom?"

"I think you solved our conundrum."

"I did, didn't I?" Irma beamed.

"What if they're bald under those hats?"

"What if only one of them is?"

"You can take the one with hair," Esme negotiated. "It was your idea."

"But it's your story."

"Hopefully they both have hair."

They sped for a mile before Esme asked Irma her opinion on the best exit to reach the farm supply.

After they settled on their route, Esme grew wistful.

"They don't even know what they're involved in," she pondered aloud. "They think they're protecting those women."

Irma joined her in solemn contemplation until they reached the farm supply outlet.

The white van was parked way in back, past the main parking lot, past the customer pickup area, by the dumpsters and the loading dock and stacks of cardboard boxes flattened for recycling.

Frankie was sitting in the driver's seat immersed in the screen on his phone. He didn't notice the girls until they were standing next to the rolled-down window.

They said hello in Spanish and he said he spoke English.

He did, but as Esme and Irma introduced themselves and engaged in some small talk about the weather and how busy he had been, Frankie sounded like he was throwing words he made up in a mumble between the clear words that had definitions. He drew out each of his invented words with a long last syllable, filling the air with noise while he stalled to find the next real word.

"You looking for work?" he said, and wasn't kidding. He took his work seriously.

"No," Esme took the lead since she didn't have to worry about translating her thoughts on the fly. "You're Frankie, yes?"

"Frankie Friend," he asserted.

Esme and Irma skimmed each other for tips on how to react.

"Frankie Friend?" Esme confirmed.

"Yeah."

He buried himself back into his phone. He had no use for someone not looking for work.

Esme and Irma couldn't come to a decision. They were frozen next to the van, which didn't bother Frankie Friend.

"Okay, then," Esme decided. "But if you call yourself Frankie Friend, shouldn't you wear a pinstriped suit and a fedora?"

"What?"

"Do you know 'Rocking the Boat'? 'Luck Be a Lady'? Anything from *Guys and Dolls*?"

Frankie waved her off and went back to his phone.

"How about ripping off a bunch of housekeepers," Esme got his attention. "Holding them hostage in an icky old motel while they work in a brand new resort for free."

"Who are you?" he glared at Esme. "You told me your names, but you never told me why you're here."

"We were about to," Esme explained. "But then you told us your name."

He needed more.

"That sent us down the whole 'Frankie Friend' path," Irma tried to accommodate him. "Really threw us off course."

"We're working on a story for our school paper," Esme put them back on track.

"The high school?" Frankie smiled.

"Yes," Esme replied.

"My son goes there. You know Emanuel?"

"What's his last name?"

"Ah," Frankie wagged his finger. "Nice try, reporter."

"I wasn't..." Esme didn't bother finishing the prelude and jumped right to the reason. "It's a big school."

"But not a lot of Emanuels, I bet. Not like I said his name was Jose, or Steve."

"What grade is he in?" Irma asked.

"Freshman."

"We don't know him," both girls said in unison.

Frankie laughed.

"Even if he was older," he pulled out of his laughter but a smile remained. "You're out of his league."

Esme redirected the conversation before she and Irma had a chance to be disgusted.

"So what's the deal with the housekeepers?"

"Why do you want to know?"

"We told you."

"This isn't the kind of thing you see in a high school paper," he gravitated back to a serious tone.

"Maybe it should be," Esme said.

"There are people with lots of money involved. Lots of power."

"I know," Esme exhaled. "Boy, do I know."

"Do you know how bad it is for these women?" Irma asked Frankie.

"I have a feeling," he said. "If they fly people in from the Philippines to do a job my mother does for next to nothing, it must be pretty bad."

"Show him the receipt," Irma urged Esme.

Esme complied, and Frankie studied it.

"Sucks," he offered as he handed it back.

"That's it?" Irma was incredulous.

"Why don't you call ICE?" he fired back.

Irma looked at Esme as if repeating the question.

"Because I want to know who the rats are before the ship sinks and they all jump off," she defended herself.

Irma was impressed.

Esme was emboldened.

"Good luck with that," Frankie scoffed. "The big rats ain't even on the ship. I'm as high as you're gonna get."

"So why aren't you more careful?" Esme asked.

"You got opinions on how I do business?"

"Edwin and Oso."

"Oh. So?"

He giggled over his accidental word play.

The girls did not.

"Oso," he repeated, as if to say 'get it?'

"They're not exactly intimidating," Esme interrupted his moment of pride.

"They work cheap and they won't snitch," Frankie consented to an explanation. "The ladies are scared enough already. But I still give them mean looks when I pick them up and drop them off, and when I deliver the checks."

"Checks," Esme sneered.

"Why did you take this job?" Irma asked him.

"This job?" Frankie was undaunted. "My job is always the same. Find people to fill other jobs."

"Why did you find people for this one?"

"This is my office," he slapped the dashboard of the van, then gestured out to the lot littered with cardboard scraps and plastic tatters. "This is my office building. You think I can afford to turn anything down?"

"That's such an easy answer," Esme rejoined.

"Because it's true, and true forever, past and future. Every job I have is shitty, but people line up because they have no choice."

"There's a difference between a shitty job and an evil one."

"Maybe. But people take them for the same reasons."

Esme was growing exasperated.

"You should learn more about the agency that called you," she said.

"Is this when you tell me about them?"

"They won't talk to me."

"Good. I don't want to lie when I say I know nothing."

Esme and Irma looked at each other to see if either had anything more to say, but both appeared to have exhausted all their moves.

They noticed a dusty man by the loading dock waiting his turn.

Frankie saw him, too.

"Excuse me, girls. I have another client looking for a shitty job. Go work on your story, go to school Monday."

They abandoned their space by the van and the man took their place.

"Is there anyone else for someone to blame?" Irma asked as they walked back to Esme's car.

"That's it," she answered. "We're at the bottom of the chain."

"I'm not certain it's a chain," Irma said. "More like a circle."

Esme reflected on her metaphor while they lowered themselves into their seats.

"Maybe a chain in the shape of a circle," she played with a combination of their images.

"A daisy chain," Irma played along.

But their lightness couldn't hold. The day had delivered too much disappointment.

When she dropped off Irma at the Art and Wine Festival where her mother was selling homemade jewelry, Esme thanked her for being by her side.

Irma thanked Esme for trying to do right, whatever the reason might be.

The sun was setting through Esme's window when she surrendered to a lack of motivation. She listed her discoveries from that morning and afternoon, but blending them into the story would have to wait. She had modest hopes for the next day.

Her phone buzzed.

Blake's name appeared atop a text bubble.

"I just saw Dorothy."

Her first response was to hope he was wrong.

"How do you know?"

"Her nametag."

She started to ask him to describe her, but backspaced out of that bubble. He wasn't taunting her, but she had a hard time seeing it otherwise. She didn't know what to say.

"And...?" she finally wrote.

"Do you want me to give her a message?" he asked.

She had even less of an idea what to say to that. All she could think of was an excuse.

"No," she wrote. "I need to keep my distance."

"You do?"

"I can't do my job well if I get too close."

That's what she learned that day, she felt like typing into the story she was working on: How important it is to build a wall around yourself.

She might have said so to Blake if he pressed her, but all he said was "OK."

# CHAPTER 8

For her first trip to the trendy brunch spot downtown, Esme would have preferred to go with Irma, and maybe Daisy, but Josh was probably better suited to take her there. He looked like the kind of person who would spend a Sunday on its patio and spend the kind of money they charged for eggs. It was his treat, but it was her guilt that sealed the invitation.

"Looking forward to this afternoon," he texted her that Sunday morning.

She was about to ask him if he texted her by accident, if he meant to contact someone from the construction project or, she considered teasing him, some other girl. Only while weighing the possibility of including the joke about the other girl did she remember the text he had sent earlier that week, and her reply to it, which was quickly buried under a stream of ensuing messages and her preoccupation with truth, justice, and application essays.

She scrolled back in time and found their exchange, then stripped the message she was drafting of all confusion and wisecracks and simply wrote "Me too" while wondering if her absent-mindedness had to do with her obsessiveness, or if the charm she could have sworn he oozed in the construction office was short-lived, if that perceived perfection was cookie-cutter rather than statuesque. She warmed to the invitation as the hour approached. Some free time at a hot spot with a date straight off the UCLA brochure would be a soothing diversion from the housekeeping traffic. If he turned out to be boring, all the better. She could enjoy the food more.

The restaurant bordered the town square, so while the open-air storefront faced a steady stream of passing pedestrians and vehicles, the park with its gazebo and hundred-year-old trees were just beyond the flow. The brunch rush had slowed from its peak in the late morning, as

Josh figured it would, so they only had a ten minute wait, which they used to review the basics of their first meeting.

How school was going.

How the hotel was coming.

When they were seated, Josh was proud to announce he had delivered on securing an interview with the construction manager for Esme's article.

"Oh…" she plotted a way to break it to him that she killed the piece once Dorothy's letter arrived. "My editor pulled it. Not enough room in the next edition. Sorry."

"That's okay," he assured her. "He'll be relieved."

"And now everything between us is off the record," she further lightened the bright side. "There is no record. Just you and me hanging out."

"On that note," he fidgeted. "I hope you don't think it's pervy that I asked you out."

"If I was thirty and you were thirty-four…"

"Thirty-five," he corrected her.

"Thirty-five," she complied. "Nobody would care."

"But we're not. And you are seventeen, right?"

"Yes."

"Good."

"That's where you draw the line," she verified. "No sixteen-year-olds."

He took her jab in stride.

"If you were sixteen, I'd lean way back all through the meal," he said, then showed her how.

She appreciated the effort.

"But," he sat normally. "We're not in our thirties."

"It's brunch," she shrugged.

"And you're more mature than most of the people I go to college with."

"I've been planning my future since I was eleven."

"Has anyone told you that's sad?"

"Lots of people have told me it's sad."

"Then I won't."

"Thank you."

Their server arrived, introduced herself and the specials, and took their drink order.

"So..." Esme set the agenda after their server left. "Engineering."

"You interested?"

"Maybe. I'm afraid it might be one of those things that sounds better than it is."

"I've seen that happen. Every so often at a party someone gets all truthy after a couple of beers and admits they hate their major, but they're three years into it and seventy-five grand in debt, so they stick with it. Forward march."

"They'll make a lot of money."

"That's what they tell themselves."

"That's why they chose it."

"But you're smarter than that," he offered as a sincere compliment.

"Maybe," she allowed. "But I also think my math talent may be maxed out at high school Calculus."

"Honors Calculus, I assume."

She gestured as if to say "naturally", and he responded in kind.

"On the flip side," he reverted back to verbal communication. "I also know people who keep changing majors hoping for that spark. They treat the course catalogue like a dating app."

"For the money they're paying, why not?"

"You end up spending even more by getting bored too easily."

"Only if your changes involve extremely different departments."

"It's good to be discerning, but I wouldn't hold out for the perfect path."

"So you're not all that into being an engineer," she prodded.

He offered a congratulatory nod for seeing through him.

"Following your bliss has its limits," he added. "I get it. It's nice when it happens. But if you think you're doing something wrong just because you're not constantly in love with your work, you're in for a long, discouraging life."

"You settled, then."

"That's one way to put it."

"You gave up on true love and married that girl with the nice personality."

"I think we've burned through the relationship analogy."

"That's your opinion. I'm still into it."

"Real romance, with a person, deserves way more caution," he insisted, "because it has the power to make everything else more bearable."

He ended his statement on a flirty note.

"Even being an engineer?" she played tone deaf.

Josh reverted back to elder mode.

"I may lack passion for my work," he said. "And maybe I even wish once in a while that I found something more inspiring. But I don't hate it, and I'll never be disappointed."

The server brought their iced teas. After ordering their food, Esme stuck to questions about campus life for the rest of their time at the table, allowing him to play mentor some more, but through lurid stories of campus debauchery rather than advice.

The stories kept coming as they strolled through the park after their meal. The one about the buttoned-up biochemistry major who broke so free on cans of White Claw one night he used an electric carving knife to cut the cast off his leg and use it as a mock sword had Esme wondering if the same kind of curbed energy was fueling the rush of stories spilling from Josh, that he was only cocksure on the job, and as socially awkward out of the office as the chem student was out of the lab. Or he was feeling sheepish about their confessional brunch and was overcompensating. Maybe she made him nervous. She pondered going in for a kiss to make him stop. That would be her first time, though, and she didn't want to waste it. Plus he had been talking so much, his breath was probably bad.

Instead she debated out loud whether to keep UCLA on her wish list thanks to his tales of depravity.

"I could tell you some inspiring stories involving wonderful students," he said. "But you can find plenty of those in the catalogue."

"Someone has to tell the idiots' story."

"That's right," Josh raised a fist.

She admitted it would take about a thousand more stories for her to reconsider his alma mater's place in her heart. Her choice of words helped her realize she was more interested in his school than in him.

They hugged goodbye when they reached Esme's car, and agreed to hang out again sometime in such a polite manner that it was doubtful they would.

When she was back in her room, she reveled in doing homework, in playing to her strengths. Being good at something felt great. It was a feeling she had taken for granted as far back as she could remember. She was not used to floundering, and the fail was happening in her first major attempt at doing good for someone else, which was troubling. She stuck to book work, Calculus and AP History notes, and ignored her laptop, where her sunken story of Dorothy rested somewhere inside of it.

The sun filtered through the blinds in her window by the time she finished studying. She shut her History text with a satisfying thud and laid back to study the fading lines of light beaming through the air above her. She heard her father tinkering around the backyard, his signal that he had struck a deal with the voices and was fully invested in the tangible world for the time being. The sounds coaxed her off the bed and toward the window. She angled the slats of the blinds to look downward into the yard and saw that he was tending to the birdcages, which meant he was not only present, but had a gig.

He was like a dad who traveled a lot for business, only he never left town. Maybe that's why he acted so casually when he would return, no matter how much time had passed, as though he had always been there. He was often just down the street. Or maybe he associated serenity with the normalcy he wanted to maintain. Whatever his motive, he greeted her with the usual lack of fanfare when she went into the yard to see him, even though she hadn't seen him in nearly two weeks.

"Hello there, Ez," he said.

She loved that he had his own nickname for her, but would have also loved a little "I missed you" energy when he came back from a trip.

He was loading two birds each into the portable cages, which were cat carriers, the kind with suitcase handles on top.

"A gig on a Sunday night?"

He was cupping a white dove in his hands, guiding it into the carrier, his grip tight enough that it wouldn't escape, gentle enough not to hurt it.

"A real nice one," he said as much to the dove as to Esme.

He placed the bird in a cage where a fellow dove was already bobbing behind the bars.

"Sunset service for a local church," he addressed her directly as he latched the carrier door. "Lots of old members, so they lose a lot of them every year. One of the families has that walnut orchard on the hill behind Walmart, and every spring they head up there to read the names of those they lost. I hand a bird to everyone who's willing to hold one, and every time the pastor reads a name, somebody rings a bell and someone releases a bird."

"That does sound nice."

"Want to help?"

"Love to."

"Then start loading," he gestured to the stack of doves.

She grabbed a carrier in each hand and walked them through the gate to his van. On her way back, she took a detour into the house to tell her Mom she was joining Dad.

"You two should grab a bite to eat afterwards," she suggested.

"That's a good idea."

"I don't feel like cooking," she feigned.

Esme smiled at her, but her Mom didn't look up in order to keep a straight face. Esme kept a mocking close eye on her as she went back out to join her Dad.

"One thing..." her Dad said when she came to collect more cages.

"What's that?"

"Don't expect me to be profound."

"When have I ever expected that?"

"It's not so much you," he shook off his previous statement. "I just feel like when I get back from negotiations, everyone thinks I've got answers."

"To what questions?"

"The big ones. As if I've been to the other side and glimpsed the eternal."

"You've been down the block in the back of a van."

He touched his nose and pointed at her as if she guessed the right answer in a game of charades.

They finished loading the back of that very van with birds in cat carriers, the back that also functioned as a tool shed for "Warren Lockhart: Handyman at Large", and a conference room for his dialogues disguised as monologues to anyone within earshot.

When they were a few minutes from reaching the hill, Esme glanced back at the birds and considered those other uses for the space.

"Is Andrea still there?" she asked.

"She stormed out," he replied. "Sore loser."

"Where does she go?"

"Not to the other side. No way."

"Seems like she would think it's boring here."

"She does. If there weren't so many places to drink, she wouldn't bother. A winery is just a bar to her. She's convinced I think it's boring, too. That's why she keeps coming back."

"She's beautiful, right?"

"She's a combination of every beautiful woman I ever met."

Esme hesitated. She saw the hill up ahead. The walnut orchard was in bloom, thick with white flowers that made the trees look like giant popcorn balls.

"Don't take this the wrong way," she said. "But if she's so hot, why doesn't she move on? Why is she so determined to ruin your life?"

"She's getting older."

"The voice in your head is getting older? Maybe it'll just die then."

"That's what she's afraid of. She's what happens when you base your life on your looks."

They reached the driveway and climbed its curves through the popcorn trees.

"If she's all about the physical," Esme wondered. "How did she get so clever?"

"She's not."

"She keeps you in negotiations for days."

"She's stubborn. Clever's got nothing to do with it."

Esme thought of synonyms for stubborn as they climbed the hill.

Determined, unwavering, persistent, tenacious.

All of them sounded more positive. She didn't like the word stubborn.

The service was set up in the backyard of the house, facing away from the Walmart and its surrounding parking lot, looking instead toward the other side of the hill, where more hills rolled into the distance seasoned with oak trees, an occasional home, another orchard a few peaks away, and vineyards rising from most of the rest. The majority of the church flock stood on the lawn, aside from a half-dozen particularly old members granted folding chairs. The pastor preached from atop three steps that led to a deck, telling stories that featured those being memorialized. When he was done, attendees came forward one at a time with some additional tales. During the third yarn, the pastor approached Esme's father and instructed him to distribute the birds before they ran out of sunlight. Esme and her Dad obliged, hauling over the cages and pulling out one dove at a time, making the rounds on the lawn with a bird in hand, approaching anyone who exhibited a flicker of interest to give them a dove along with instructions on how to hold it.

"Don't worry if they struggle. That's natural. Hold firm. They'll settle down."

The storyteller on the steps wrapped up as the doves started to snare everyone's attention. The pastor reclaimed the top spot while a woman stood behind him with a large hand bell that she held upright against her chest, as though waiting for her cue as the low note on the far end of a bell choir.

After the pastor read the first name, she swept the bell outward for a single note before drawing it back against herself to stop the vibration. The bird holders were unsure who should go first. Someone finally took the lead and released their dove to scattered chuckles. After the second name was read and the bell tolled, two people let go of their birds at once, to even more chuckles. By the third name, the group found their rhythm, and one bird at a time was set free for each bell tone onward.

With the pattern established and everyone comfortable in their role, Esme was able to enjoy the ceremony. She didn't recognize any of the names, but was touched nonetheless by the reading of them. At times it was clear that a widow or widower of the name being read was the person releasing their bird. The tears in their eyes would turn to wonder when they let it go and followed the flight.

Most of the birds circled back around the house rather than out toward the hills, since that was the direction of their home cage. Several birds were still in hand after the last name was read and bell rung. The pastor raised his arms and everyone with a holdout understood what to do.

The small flock fluttered above them in chaos for a couple of seconds before finding their places and flying in relative order toward home.

"Let's join them," Esme's Dad whispered to her.

They stopped at the twenty-four hour diner on their way. In spite of the growing tourism, restaurant options on a Sunday night were still limited. They may have ended up there anyway, as it was her favorite place to go with him when she was little.

"You still into the cake batter milkshake?" he asked as the menu jogged his memory.

"Not since I threw one up on a road trip to girl scout camp."

"I never heard about that."

"I begged the troop leader not to tell anyone."

"So what'll it be, then?" he went off menu and tried to recall something without a prompt. "The clown pancakes?"

"They're supposed to be bunny rabbits."

"Those are ears? I thought they were one of those balloon animal hats."

"You never noticed the nose and whiskers?"

"I was more into the construction of the pancake, not the decorations."

"Once a contractor, always a contractor," she said before wondering if she should have, as it did seem to take a small bite out of her Dad.

"Hey," he thought of something to say to replace that part of himself. "I saw the kid from across the street pass by when I was in negotiations."

"So?"

"You ever talk to him anymore?"

"I don't think he speaks anymore."

"How refreshing."

She admired how her father was always so candid about his condition, but when his transparency turned to jokes, she was never comfortable laughing at them.

"You know," he gave her permission. "Voices."

"I get it."

"Sorry," he backed off into the original subject. "You two used to have such a good time together."

"A long time ago."

"I guess."

"Like eight years ago, maybe ten."

"I know that takes up a big chunk of your timeline, Ez," he held his hands a yard apart to demonstrate. "But that's about this much of mine."

He brought his hands within inches of each other.

She didn't mind speculating on how young she was when it was her idea, but she resented reminders, so she reviewed the menu with phony concentration.

Many of the dishes from her childhood were still available, which she found charming, but they didn't make her any more hungry.

"I think I'll just have something to drink and maybe some fries."

"You sure?"

"I had brunch today," she announced with mock flourish.

"Kids are into brunch these days?"

"I was on a date with someone a little older."

"Anyone I know?"

"I said *a little* older."

"He likes brunch."

"Early twenties."

She noticed her Dad wince.

"He goes to UCLA," she added, as if that would make a difference.

"Where'd you meet him?"

"Through a story for the paper. He's working on the new hotel project."

Her Dad glared.

"The one near the golf course?"

"Yes," she wondered why it mattered.

"Doing what?" he dared to ask.

"This and that," she proceeded with caution. "He's on some kind of paid internship."

The server arrived to welcome them and take a drink order, but her Dad didn't appear to notice.

"Dad?"

"Hmm?" he resurfaced.

"Something to drink?"

"Water," he said as though in dire need of it.

When the server left, Esme asked him what was wrong.

"I'll bet they have him making very thorough sweeps of the site and compiling very detailed reports."

"That seems to be part of it," she confirmed. "Is there something wrong with that?"

"Not necessarily. Unless you work for that particular company."

"How so?"

"They're not going to pay the sub-contractors for the final phase of the project."

"They're not?"

"That's what they do. That's what his reports are for. They're building their case."

"How do you know?"

"Because they did it to me and I lost my business because I was stupid enough to fight them."

Esme joined her father in dismay. It was his turn to talk her back into consciousness.

"I didn't even lose my case," he said. "But it cost more than if I had just let that last paycheck go. That's how they get away with it."

"Is that why…" she stopped short of completing the question.

"No," he answered anyway. "I can't pin the voices on them. Not completely. But it didn't help."

Esme spent the rest of their evening together in a contemplative frenzy, barely able to pay attention to events outside herself.

Most of her time at school the next day was the same. She avoided people as much as possible since her company was useless. All she thought about was confronting Josh: what she would ask, how he might reply, what she could say in turn. She wondered if this is what it was like when her Dad heard voices. During the final two periods of her schedule she repeatedly reminded herself to stay calm.

She didn't have much time before rehearsal, they were starting full tech run-throughs that week, but it was all the time she needed.

Josh wasn't in the office. Rather than wait, she marched into the construction zone and searched for him. Two different men told her she wasn't allowed in the area without a hard hat. She asked the first one to get Josh for her, and told the second one she wasn't leaving until she talked to Josh.

By the time he appeared from inside the frame of the building, hard hat in place, word was out about the crazy girl. He tried to guide her toward the trailer before she spoke, but she would not budge.

"Do you know what you're doing?" she asked.

"I'll answer that!" a nearby worker called out.

Josh acknowledged him with a good-natured smirk before turning back to Esme.

"Can you at least keep your voice down?" he pleaded.

She complied.

"Do you know they're going to use your reports to avoid paying these people?" she said softly enough to avoid causing a riot.

"What are you talking about?"

"My Dad lost everything thanks to the people you work for. Maybe even his sanity."

"I'm sorry."

She couldn't tell if he was playing dumb or genuinely ignorant.

"So is that the deal?" she pressed him.

"If it is, I swear I didn't know."

"Well," she settled down. "Now you do."

"Thank you."

He seemed to think the conversation was over.

"What are you going to do about it?" she wouldn't let him go.

"What do you want me to do? Quit?"

"No, because they would just find another suck-up to do what you do."

"Then what?"

"Make sure it doesn't happen."

"How?"

"You're smart. You got into a hot engineering program that takes like a 4.8 and a 1500 on the SAT. Figure it out."

Josh took a long, slow breath and looked ready to surrender.

"What's in it for me?" he asked.

Esme needed a moment, during which Josh realized he needed to change course.

"I'm joshin'," he claimed.

"You're what?"

"Joshing."

"Does that mean joking?"

"Yes. You've never heard that expression?"

"If I did, it didn't stick."

"It was a big thing in my family when I was kid, since, you know. My name. I would tell one of those goofy kid jokes and they would say I was joshing."

"And you let them."

"Whatever, Esme. Point being, I was joking when I asked what's in it for me."

"No, you weren't."

"I was."

"Not selling your soul. That's in it for you."

"I told you..."

"Save it," she held up her hand and walked away.

Nobody could hear them anymore, but her actions inspired whoops and clucks from the crew.

"Do what you want, Josh," she turned to face him, taking advantage of the noise to muffle one last shot. "It's too late to save my Dad, so why should I care? Why should anyone care about anyone else?"

She spun back around to applause from every story of the frame. Since the men didn't hear what she had said, they were cheering her movements. Their leering contributed to why she was rattled by the noise rather than flattered. But her hypocrisy was the main reason. "What's in it for me" was a guiding principle in her life. She felt exposed, undeserving of an ovation. From a distance, the moment may have looked like a daydream come true, but up close, in her head, she was gripped by the kind of anxiety that usually visited in the middle of the night.

As soon as she reached the driver's seat of her car, she called Zack.

She was relieved to hear him answer so she could avoid stammering out a message on voice mail.

He was glad to hear from her.

"I should have called sooner," she said. "I shouldn't have waited at all. I should have told you the day Irma and I came to see you."

"You know some of the people involved," he gathered.

"Yes."

"Then I get it," he assured her. "It's not that easy."

She provided a quick summary of the situation. He knew where The Riverbed was, and said they would round up everyone within twenty-four hours.

She thanked him, and he thanked her.

During rehearsal, for the first time Esme wished she could switch places with the girl playing her dream role. Not for any of the reasons she would have imagined when the show was first announced, and only for one scene. All she wanted to do was grip that plywood machine gun and pretend to saturate the back of the stage with pinpoints of light. They rehearsed it until the crew managed to synchronize the lights with the sound of rapid fire. When they finally got it right, any envy she may have felt gave way to joy. That was her up there, even if she wasn't center stage. She was the one lighting up the world, righting a wrong, firing at will. That was her, not a character.

She enjoyed the spectacle so much she kept losing track of the steps, and had to catch up with the rest of the cast on the first available beat.

# CHAPTER 9

The next edition of the paper wasn't due to be published for another three weeks. In the meantime, Esme wrote a straight news report covering the raid on The Riverbed that Daisy posted on their website before law enforcement fed the story to other media outlets through a press release. Mr. Hawley was positive this was the first time the school paper had broken a story concerning an off-campus event. And though they promoted that achievement, most people seemed to rely on their preferred news sites to learn about the tale of the two hotels.

Esme received some adulation. The local paper featured her in an article about her article, and the local network news affiliate gave her credit when they reported on the story, all of which led her to believe more people read about her covering the bust than her actual coverage of the bust.

"Is it breaking news if nobody reads it?" she lamented to Daisy.

"People don't come to our website for that sort of thing."

"For news?"

Daisy chalked one up for Esme, but proceeded with an explanation anyway.

"They come for the student perspective on things already happening. We're young voices, not a news crawl."

Which was why they were having a lunch meeting in the journalism room, to discuss Esme's follow-up feature documenting her discovery and pursuit of the story. Daisy maintained that the ethical squishiness of Esme's tactics prevented them from presenting her work as investigative reporting, but agreed to an editorial spin.

"You have to filter all the moves you made and the tricks you played through an opinion, through a theme you develop," was her exact directive.

Esme agreed, and already had a theme in mind. She was leaning toward the title "Circle of Denial", and wanted to focus on what she called the Accountability Shuffle, the dance of being passed from one entity to the next when she tried to figure out who was ultimately in charge of hiring indentured servants to clean rooms at a multimillion dollar luxury resort in an affluent zip code.

Daisy liked the angle, and blessed it as they crumpled their lunch bags and wrappers and took turns trying to toss them into the large garbage can at the edge of the computer cove.

"I'm really happy with how this is turning out," Daisy said as her first throw, a plastic sandwich bag weighed down with a quarter of her turkey and Swiss, flopped off the rim and onto the floor. "For a while I wasn't sure I could be your friend anymore."

Esme wadded up a Hot Cheetos bag and lined up her shot.

"What exactly changed your mind?"

She let the wad fly, but it was too light and landed well short.

"Your reaction to the breaking news story not getting hits," Daisy said as she chose her next projectile.

"I didn't take that very well," Esme reminded her.

"No," Daisy went with half a mozzarella stick. "But you were bugged that the story wasn't gaining traction. It wasn't all about you. And when you seemed uncomfortable with the praise being heaped on you, I fell in love all over again."

The cheese landed dead center. Daisy celebrated.

"I wasn't that uncomfortable," Esme admitted.

She was down to her last tossable, the brown paper bag that once held them all.

"A little was enough," Daisy tried to block her shot, but missed as her hand swiped through the air. "It was a sign of life."

Daisy's words meant a lot to Esme, but as her article took shape, they started to sound sarcastic whenever Esme recalled them.

Each sentence she wrote seemed to pump another blast of self-regard into the piece. She felt as though the real theme starting to surface was asking for a pat on the back for something any decent person would have done. When the vanity roared to its crest, her initial reaction was to implicate others. Guilt wasn't limited to those being fingered in her editorial, she tried to claim. We are all complicit in denying the humanity of others when we ignore their plight, even if we aren't the ones brokering the deals.

Or something along those lines.

She deleted a dozen versions of the same sermon. Casting a wider net didn't even fool herself, so she couldn't imagine anyone else being thrown off the scent of her ego. She was still the one holding the net, preaching while she monitored the catch. No change in wording or reshuffling of syntax would alter the tone. Her voice was draped in the pride of a person who has done something for someone else for the first time in their life.

The only way around her sermonizing was to bring in a fresh point of view, yield space to a voice she had read but not heard, the voice she had been avoiding in spite of its profound effect on her.

When Esme called the detention center, she was given the impression an Ilocano translator would be hard to come by, so she asked Blake if his aunt was available. She probably was, he said, but she lived in Colorado Springs.

She considered driving to the center on her own and making due with hand gestures and speaking loudly, as people are prone to do when trying to be understood, as if volume can compensate for lack of expression. But the drive was long and the bureaucracy thick. She didn't want to waste a trip.

Fortunately, Dorothy's case caught the attention of a reputable Immigration Attorney who was representing her pro bono, and the lawyer's office had a medley of translators on retainer. Esme contacted the office and introduced herself, explained the latest leg of her journey regarding Dorothy, and was granted access to a translator.

Her name was Hazel. She was so quiet on the drive to the detention center that Esme wondered if translators weren't allowed to speak unless they were translating, as they exchanged maybe two minutes' worth of conversation during the two hours it took to get there.

The center was a prison that had been converted when its contract was sold from one agency to another, but most of the changes seemed to be contained in the mission statement rather than the building. The detainees wore jumpsuits, security was ubiquitous and well-armed, and the visiting area separated insiders from outsiders with thick glass.

Her first time seeing Dorothy, and it was behind glass.

She felt as though she wasn't really seeing her, but a picture of her, then a video of her when she started to speak.

Hazel started doing her job and was transformed. The simple task of introducing herself to Dorothy revealed an expressiveness that was near acrobatic. The chair hardly held her as she searched for the right words to foster not only communication, but articulation.

Esme didn't feel articulate at first. All she could think of to say was "I'm sorry", and Hazel said it with far more conviction in her voice and remorse in her body language. Esme was so taken with the translator's sudden metamorphosis that she failed to focus on Dorothy when delivering the apology, though guilt also played a role in adding a few more seconds to the weeks she had avoided facing her.

Dorothy's age was hard to pinpoint. Esme guessed 25-35, but would not have been surprised if the correct year fell outside that range on either end, a result of strong genes and trying circumstances. She had a young voice. Her living situation had not been smile-inducing, and her job didn't require a happy face, so her reactions were rusty. When she told Hazel that she was grateful, that Esme had nothing to be sorry for, her expression remained stoic, as though folding a sheet or scrubbing a toilet. As Hazel delivered Dorothy's assurance to Esme, she seemed to want to provide Dorothy with a demonstration on how non-verbal cues work in conjunction with words, weaving the most exaggerated possible mixture of body and verbal language so that if Dorothy could emulate even a quarter of Hazel's manner, the unreadable woman behind the glass would break through.

Esme asked about the raid, what it was like from her perspective when the authorities came for them at the motel. She thought Dorothy would have a lot to say about this, and in the process might loosen up and satisfy Hazel's latent prompting to add some sensation to her words.

Maybe the events were more exciting than how Dorothy described them, and her narrow emotional range colored them gray. Maybe it really was a dull affair: a knock at the door, an officer calmly standing in the frame when she answered. No guns drawn, no raised voices. She and the other women escorted to yet another van, as though they had called for a ride and the officer was the driver who responded. Edwin and Oso in the background in handcuffs. Either way, it was not the gripping narrative Esme imagined when she heard "raid".

That last part caught her attention, though.

"Oh no," she cried. "Edwin and Oso in handcuffs."

Dorothy and Hazel gave her a lengthy look.

"Sorry," Esme spoke to their stares. "They seemed like nice guys. I talked to them once. Did they treat you okay?"

She couldn't tell from Dorothy's tone how she answered, but she appeared to nod.

"They were not mean," is how Hazel put it.

"They had never worked for that company before," Esme continued to defend Edwin and Oso.

"Maybe we could keep the focus on Dorothy," Hazel reminded her while refusing to relay her statement.

"Of course," Esme agreed, and searched for something else to say.

She came up with "How are they treating you here?"

"Decent."

Which struck Esme as an interesting word to use.

"Is that a direct translation?" she asked Hazel.

"Yes," Hazel didn't like the question.

"So there's an Ilocano word that specifically means 'decent'."

"Yes," Hazel said once again with twice the irritability.

"'Decent' as in neither good nor bad, not 'decent' as in dignified, or upstanding."

"Yes," Hazel said for the third time without charm.

"It's an inexact science, though, isn't it?" Esme pressed on. "You interpret while you translate."

"Do you want to talk to Dorothy or not?"

Esme took a pre-confessional deep breath.

"This is even harder than I thought it was going to be," she said. "I should have called ICE sooner. I should have visited sooner. Anyone else would have done this whole thing so much better."

"But you did it," Hazel relaxed and tried to help Esme do likewise.

"Look at me," Esme wasn't ready to relax. "Look at this. It's about me again. Everything ends up being about me."

Dorothy asked Hazel a question.

"She asked what's wrong," Hazel told Esme.

"Tell her whatever you want," Esme leaned back and slouched in her chair. "I'll leave it up to you and your interpretation."

Hazel said something to Dorothy, who responded while Esme waited for the results.

"Dorothy wants to know if you're making money off her story."

"In a way," Esme started to sculpt an answer. "I'm not paid up front, but it might help me get into college, which can lead to more money, depending on which college, and where I..."

"No," Hazel said to Dorothy before Esme finished, then proceeded to say something else to her while Esme glared over being interrupted.

"I told her you weren't making any money off her story," Hazel explained to Esme, who continued to glare at her.

Dorothy laughed.

Only a little, and she seemed embarrassed about it, but she laughed.

She said something to Hazel, quietly, but with a small smile left over from when she laughed.

Esme was tempted to ask "What did she say?" but waited for Hazel to tell her.

"The dream was more exciting."

Dorothy's position behind the glass suddenly seemed powerful, as if she was being protected from a public that wanted something from her. She saw how intrigued Esme was and offered an explanation that was longer than anything she had said before.

Hazel provided constant updates, piecing the dream together in real time in a much more reserved manner, sitting still in her chair, needing to concentrate more now that she no longer had to incite Dorothy into communicating.

"I had it the day we arrived here, when I finally fell asleep after the long drive, all the paperwork, and all the things they did to us when we checked in. I collapsed on the bed and dreamed that the raid was much more violent, the kind of action people think happens all the time in this sort of operation. There were more men guarding us in the motel. Big, young, professional soldiers for hire that were not going down without a fight. They were yelling instructions at one another and screaming when they were hit. Bullets ripped through the walls and windows. There was nowhere to hide. That was something different than in the movies. They couldn't crouch behind a wall and shoot back through a window. The bullets found their way through everything. They were hitting the other ladies I worked with, too. The ladies hid behind chairs and under the bed, but it didn't matter. I wondered why I wasn't scared. I was anxious, and I felt sad for them, but I didn't feel like I was in danger. I realized it was because I wasn't really there. I had excused myself before the authorities arrived. I knew what was coming. It was about time for another bad thing to happen, because bad things happen on a cycle, and I was familiar with the cycle. I don't know where I was in the dream, how I could see the whole room without being inside of it. One of the men who guarded us in real life started talking to me. I think it was Edwin. I could only hear his voice. He sounded scared, like he was about to sneeze, like he always does, but as if something more than a sneeze was coming. He asked me how that was possible, how I could see the whole room from the outside. I told him anything was possible when I take myself out of the place where time repeats itself."

Her description came to an abrupt end. She sounded like she turned a page expecting to read on, but found the rest of the pages blank.

Esme wanted to fill them in. She asked Dorothy all the questions she had wondered about, the questions that would have taken up too much space in the letters they exchanged, the questions that would have led to a series of absorbing conversations if she had been willing to find her in the hallways of the resort.

At last she found out Dorothy's family was poor, but not impoverished. Her parents provided for her and her two sisters, but that was about all they could do. Her father was a carpenter for a farmer who was constantly adding on to his house, while her mother, along with Dorothy and her sisters, worked as domestics in that same expanding house. Her family was grateful to be poor in the country rather than the city, like her aunts and uncles and cousins in Manila. And they didn't even have to labor in the fields.

She described in great detail a life in the barrios, the barangays, of farm country in the northern province of Cagayan. No tourists visit. They stick to the coasts of the southern islands. But she found beauty in the cracks that would occasionally open in the time spent staying alive.

Each skinny barangay winds through a narrow valley cupped in rolling peaks of leafy canopy under an indecisive sky always within reach of a rainstorm, the floor a checkerboard of rice fields garnished with white egrets, the water within each muddy square border either green with shoots like bouquets of flowers held upside down by people trapped underneath, or empty and lying still like reflecting pools waiting for someone to make a wish. She talked about the people being both resourceful and idle, how everyone does everything, from rice and corn farming to food preparation to building and road construction to metal fabrication to motorcycle maintenance, until the season or exhaustion helps them decide to do nothing. She called it a life lived along the edges of a busy street, a sleek minority of late model cars and SUVs weaving with a warning tap of their horns past the sputtering old majority that move like boats chugging upriver: the motorized tricycles for hire buzzing in their metal casings emblazoned with the family name, its members, and a blessing; two-wheelers huffing up to four riders in flip-flops and shorts, sometimes with a pig riding sidecar; bellowing flatbed trucks with cargo stacked high and people sprinkled on top. Dogs trot inches from traffic, sniffing for scraps in the desperate space between the doorways and the car doors speeding by, obeying their survival instinct while tempting the wheels of fate. Goats and carabao are tied alongside the shoulders between the barangays, tearing at the grass and tendrils of jungle constantly trying to take over the road. Each fleeting barrio is a splash of manufactured color: stores all selling the same array of shiny snack bags and tinted drinks; empty neon yellow and lime green plastic bottles turned into works of art, carved and peeled into mini palm fronds, stars, and spirals fastened to rusty gates and hanging from mossy cement entryways; men in garish Philippine Basketball Association jerseys or knockoff NBA jerseys; women in mismatched prints, a floral top and paisley bottom, a striped top and Hello Kitty bottom. An outdoor basketball court in every barangay, the ones surrounded by concrete pillars supporting a weather-battered roof doubling as community centers. The smell of wet grass and gasoline. The sound of karaoke and roosters crowing. No bad or good neighborhoods, just one lengthy broken-up neighborhood crammed with whatever kind of house each family can afford to build, variations on a cement box. Some are bigger, with a coat of plaster and paint, designer window frames and fixtures; some are just the box. People live in their boxes during construction, filling in the blanks with tarps and rocks. Some never finish, waking every morning to an unfulfilled dream. The third world and first world dancing together with no rhythm, water perpetually dripping from the corrugated metal roofs that slope from the top of every version of each world.

The house she and her family serviced was perched out in a rice field, creating its own peninsula, with a private road leading to it that passed under an archway brandishing the name that the farmer christened his lot, like an estate or a palace, in spite of the discouraging local history of houses jutting that far out on the murky waters left abandoned after their owners are gone. Her sisters thought it was because nobody wants to have to clean out the bottom floor after a flood, which they had to do every typhoon season. Dorothy thought it was because nobody wants to live in someone else's fantasy.

She knew she was fortunate to live and work there, rather than curled up in one of the incomplete houses in the mud below the main street, but the routine had become as stifling as the humid air that kept everything drenched in green. Some summer nights it felt more like water than air. By the time the recruiter came, she often imagined herself treading in that water, floating in the air five feet off the ground, stuck in place, arms flailing, as green as her surroundings: full of life, but jealous of those whose futures are not the same as their pasts. She had security. She needed purpose. Her longing was especially vivid when she would stare at the lightest kind of rain that hovered over the house at least once a day, a drizzle she could see, but not feel when she held her hand under it. The water only left its mark when she walked or worked in it long enough.

She heard what she wanted to hear from the recruiter. She thought she could both break free, and contribute more to their household income.

Everything was legitimate at first. They were given passports, they flew on an airplane to the states. It wasn't like those stories of people being smuggled in shipping crates. But when they arrived, their passports were taken away, their living conditions were revealed, and they were charged for the airline tickets long after they had paid them off, in addition to all the other fees attached to every part of their existence.

They slept two in a bed on a caved-in mattress that felt more like a hammock, the sloped sides forcing their bodies together. She had slept in a roomful of people her whole life, but the people had always been family. The motel bungalow smelled of greasy takeout food and cigarettes that had been belched and exhaled by decades of guests, like a school cafeteria where the kids were allowed to smoke. She drifted through her shifts at the resort knowing she was not making an impression on anyone. So many things from her country were so much smaller than the things in America: toilet paper, chickens, garbage bins. And now she felt like the smallest thing of all. She was a body pushing a cart full of towels, tissue boxes, and hand soap. She was the sound of a vacuum cleaner, the smell of cleanser. Guests would either smile politely or boss her around, if they interacted with her at all. Some would leave a cash tip on the dresser or table. Since she and her fellow captives could not send the dollars to their families or deposit them in a bank, they pooled their tips for the week and went to dinner on Saturday nights. Edwin and Oso would walk them from The Riverbed to one of the two restaurants in town, either the pizza parlor or the deli. Both places served mediocre food, and both relied on fluorescent lights and Formica for atmosphere, but it was a chance to get out, to be served, to sit someplace for an hour that was not intimidating like the resort, or infested like the bungalow. They would not talk much. Maybe a story about an exceptionally nasty guest from the past week. For the most part they ate in silence. They were eager to move past this mistake and forget everything about it, including each other.

The routine made Dorothy numb, but not enough to blunt the memory of her family. She would have agreed to keep working for no pay if she could only contact them. She had escaped a pattern that frustrated her for one that drained her. Dullness buried every other emotion but grief. Months of work at the resort narrowed her field of vision to what was in front of her at any given moment. Nothing was worth remembering until she saw Esme conducting that interview with Trudy.

Having reached the part where their lives intersected, she took the opportunity to ask Esme what her side of the junction was like.

Esme was ashamed to share. She had everything, but wanted more. She stalled and insisted she had more questions for Dorothy.

If she was sure she wouldn't keep in touch with any of the women she came with.

Yes.

If she felt the least bit sorry for Edwin and Oso.

No.

If she had a pet back in the Philippines.

No.

Dorothy smiled when she said so.

"Why are you smiling?" Esme asked.

"Don't be embarrassed for having a nice life," she said. "I would like to hear about it."

Esme indulged her.

She summarized a life of childhood and teenage ambition to a woman who had nothing and worked for nothing. For all the time Esme had spent grooming her image, she had never talked about herself out loud. Every move was made to be written down when application season opened. She was tempted to invoke her father. The possibility of using her father's struggle as part of a personal statement had never crossed her mind for long, since she had yet to sit down and compose one. But here she was, in need of some conflict to spice up a life that had no story, only accomplishments. Her father's problems had not really created any for her. He was always careful to keep them away from Esme, so diligent about working his way through them, she decided it would be profane to use him as a plot device in her biography. He would probably accept the role, given how encouraging he was, and how transparent about his condition, but she couldn't accept his imaginary offer.

Exploiting her mother's conflicts with the academic community would be more palatable, but less useful. Maybe if her Mom had been shut out due to her work on the psychology of poverty or the role of race in the creation of wealth, but a debate over whether meteors or volcanoes killed the dinosaurs was unlikely to enhance the emotional appeal of her story.

She concluded her one-minute memoir and tossed the day back to Dorothy by asking permission to tell her story in the next edition.

She granted it.

Esme wrote down her cell number and passed the paper to Dorothy through the slot at the bottom of the window.

"Call me anytime," she encouraged her.

"Thank you," said Dorothy.

"No, thank you."

"For what?"

"You saved my article."

Esme delivered the line like a dancer in a musical, big and broad, so everyone present would understand she was trying to be funny, even if they didn't think she was.

They got it, but she suspected their appreciation had little to do with her delivery, and more to do with how much the line was based on the truth.

When she was back in her room, Esme deleted the whole document she had been working on without even opening it.

She kept herself out of the new draft and let Dorothy's story unfold.

That was the most important thing Esme had over the other media outlets, more so than breaking the news before them. There was the raid, and there were the circumstances that led to it, but most of all there was a person she wanted everyone to meet.

Daisy was delighted to get to know her. She wanted to make her the centerpiece of our next issue, so she ran it by the all the editors of every section for our opinion, and we were also pleased to meet her.

Some of our readers were, too.

Others gave Dorothy a chilly reception, though we doubted they actually read about her.

"Stop getting so political," was a common rebuke in the emails and comments. "You're a high school paper."

"Your agenda is showing."

"The liberal brainwashing starts in high school now instead of college."

"Any friend of yours is an enemy of America."

"Cool story. Now go back to where you came from."

As much as Esme was rooting for Dorothy to get a T visa and out of detention, she was glad that in the meantime the facility prevented access to the verbal venom being sprayed at her.

Not much of the sloganeering was directed at Dorothy explicitly. Esme rarely took any of it personally, either. The grumpy flock seemed to be cursing an idea more than any one person.

"I thought I kept ideas out of it," Esme lamented.

"People hunt for them," Daisy swore.

What bothered Daisy more was the relative lack of interest from any direction. The responses, both positive and negative, were minimal compared to the initial story they broke, and for that matter marginal compared to pieces they ran on dress codes and parking permits.

Esme was growing used to his kind of disappointment: pulling off a beautiful maneuver with a high degree of difficulty, sticking the landing, and receiving nothing but polite applause, if not silence, for the effort. Dorothy's story was engrossing, and her writing had done it justice. Of both she was convinced.

She had used all five senses to detail the setting of Dorothy's home: the humidity, the grit, the scent of fish and mud, the loud voices and soft breezes, the tasty food that relies more on bitter than sweet, and the landscape determined to turn everything green. She added layers of emotion; not only Dorothy's restlessness, but her family's dismay, their questioning of themselves upon learning of her dissatisfaction, their wonder over whether they were wrong to be content with a life their daughter dismissed. Esme contrasted Dorothy's exhilaration at touching down in the United States with the horror of discovering the job was not as advertised and no less terrifying than finding out the call was coming from inside the house, or the children were in the attic, or the corpse was in the basement. And when she contacted her family after the raid, none of them ever said "I told you so." They were happy and relieved to hear from her. They told her in quivering voices that gave away their tears how much they loved her and missed her.

Before the final draft was due for publication, Esme offered to pay Hazel for a translation so she could run it by Dorothy. Hazel did it for free. Esme drove to the center by herself, slid the pages through the glass, and watched Dorothy read her story. She also brought a note she translated on her own that encouraged Dorothy to feel free to suggest any changes. She waived her freedom to edit and praised Esme's writing in her standard stoic manner, aside from the tear that ran down her cheek. She let it flow, only wiping it away after she agreed to let Esme take her picture.

Esme swiped a copy of the new edition for delivery to the detention center, but wasn't able to follow through until after the gauntlet of reactions had accumulated. Finally delivering it served as a consoling reminder that the only reader who really mattered was Dorothy, and she approved. She was going to need a while to read the English version, but the sight of her life playing out amongst all the other stories overwhelmed her far more than seeing the earlier draft. Pictures of students playing softball, swimming, posing with food items from their lunch bags for an article on nutrition, holding for close-ups that accompanied their answers to the poll question of what they planned to do over the summer, mugging for candid shots during club day in the quad, and there was Dorothy featured in the middle of them all. She shed no tears as she leafed through the pages, only smiled.

But people had already heard the short version of her story, and that was enough for them. They had moved on, even though the follow-up was far better than the original. They only had so much attention to spend on any one topic.

Esme's mother thought there was something deeper scaring away an audience when it came to widening the space of the subject matter.

"We like small worlds," she told her daughter in the kind of tone Esme always imagined her using in front of a class, filling that tone with high-value vocabulary words and splashy metaphors to hold the room. "But at the same time we like to think of our worlds as big, so we don't like it when someone tears at that fabric and forces us to see the void, and how small we really are."

They were out for an early pizza after school at her mother's insistence, thanks to a sense of maternal duty. She had been watching Esme realize that her work was not going to make the ground move, and she felt obligated to say something. As if to wink at Esme's suspicions over the classroom parallels in their conversation, Lupe used her job to bring the worlds metaphor down to earth.

"It's like students from tiny high schools when they get to college. They go from running a place to wondering if they belong in a place."

Her mother the professor downed the last sip of agua fresca in her cup and sucked in some ice.

"Some of them figure it out," she chewed on the ice. "The ones with skills. Others, I don't know, I think they got by on charm. They showed initiative at a high school where not many students have it, so the teachers cheered them on."

"Can I get you a refill?" Esme stood up with an empty cup of her own.

"I know you hate it when I chew ice," Lupe handed hers over. "Almost as much as when I try to be profound."

"I don't mind," she took the cup. "That much."

Lupe thought Esme was being funny and nodded her approval. But Esme really did appreciate the effort. Her Mom was trying to make her feel better based solely on the most flattering part of what happened. Her walk to the beverage station felt long, like a pilgrimage. She was too ashamed to divulge the part where she waited several weeks to call someone who could save Dorothy because she wanted to be a savior, and a freshman at Stanford.

What her Mom said about worlds shrinking and expanding was on her mind much later when she woke up after an hour's sleep around midnight in the arms of anxiety, rolling through every position that offered a moment of comfort, taking deep breaths, and reminding herself how lucky she was. She was certain if she fell out of bed she would fall forever.

Holding fast to her mattress, she reached a conclusion that the tepid reaction to her work was for the best. Dorothy's life was her own. She came here to help herself and the people she loved, not teach anyone anything, or tap their emotions. Esme wondered if a lesson was all she took from their relationship.

She moved past her need for attention, about as well as someone of her age and ambition could, thanks in part to the spring musical. The role she coveted ended with the rest of the show, and aside from Roxie earning a slightly louder level of applause during the curtain call, and a few more well-wishers after each performance, by a week after closing, the whole production was a solid memory only to those who acted in it, and a faint one fading fast to those who had come to see it.

But the notion that she was expecting to grow from her time with Dorothy gnawed at her, as if Dorothy was not a person, but a lecture. She didn't want to use her any more than she already had, so she decided not to include what happened between them on her college applications after all, and buried it as one of an anonymous "seven articles" included as a bullet point under the general category of "Journalism" on her list of extracurricular activities.

For the personal statement asking her to describe an event that taught her a lesson, she went with the time her father took her to a memorial service on a hill to release some doves that would fly back to their house, but for those whose loved ones were being honored, they may as well have been flying to heaven.

# CHAPTER 10

"What if your grades and test scores weren't so strong?" Irma asked Esme. "What if you didn't have all those other activities on your profile?"

They were surrounded by lights, strolling with a merry crowd on a cold winter vacation night as part of a traditional holiday display that ran through the month of December at a storied seaside resort. The two of them shuffled along with the tide of people through a temporary tunnel created by wrapping the trunks of pine trees that lined the path in strands of red and green lights, which were then strung between the branches above. They held paper cups of hot cider that Esme bought. She figured it was the least she could do since Irma had treated Esme with tickets to the light festival to celebrate her early acceptance to a couple of colleges that she never planned on attending. Esme only applied to them to gauge how well the process was playing out, to receive some good news, and to ease her mind while she waited to hear from the true objects of her desire. So far the plan was unfolding as she had hoped.

"If none of those things were true," Esme answered the question about her grades and scores and activities, "then I wouldn't have applied anywhere in the first place. I'd go to A&M, or use my Mom to get into State."

"I mean if it was borderline," Irma clarified. "If you had solid grades, decent scores, not great. If you had some campus clubs listed but didn't do anything after school. Then would you have put the Dorothy affair on your application?"

"The person you're describing doesn't seem like someone who would have caught Dorothy's eye."

Irma sighed as they emerged from the tunnel of lights.

"And instead of Journalism junior year," she extended her parallel universe, "you took a Work Experience class. And you had to write an essay for it and you decided to write about hotel jobs and Dorothy saw you there interviewing a manager. You know what I mean."

"I do," Esme admitted. "And I know what you want me to say."

"Well?"

"It was easy for me to keep off one thing thanks to all the other things."

Irma responded with an emphatic, playful nod.

"I could afford to do the right thing," Esme refined her analysis.

"That sounds more condescending than how I was thinking of it," Irma backed down.

"I've been asking myself the same question, and that's how I think of it, because you're nicer than me."

She put her free arm around Irma and kissed her cheek. They stepped outside the flow of people and found a bench that faced a lawn laced with white lights that led to a burst of colored shrubs behind it. They sat as though looking across a great valley or body of water.

Esme dragged on a sip of cider.

"Yeah," she unburdened herself during a post-sip exhale. "If I needed the Dorothy story more, I probably would have used it."

"That's okay," Irma sipped in solidarity. "I always thought you should have anyway. Dorothy would probably agree. She got her T visa out of it. Why would she mind?"

"What if she didn't get her visa?" Esme proposed, never having considered that angle before.

Irma looked mesmerized by the lights.

"Irma?"

"I'm thinking about your question," she replied without taking her eyes off the spectacle.

Esme watched it with her and waited for her answer.

"She still wouldn't mind," Irma decided. "She'd be back in the Philippines. Happy."

"She wouldn't even know I used her."

"She's here now and doesn't know you didn't use her."

"I would know."

"And I would know," Irma said. "Because we tell each other everything."

"We do," Esme agreed. "Eventually."

She made a move to put her head on Irma's shoulder, but Irma did the same, and they bumped heads instead.

They straightened up into their original positions and gazed at the lights as though nothing happened.

"Shall we try it again?" Esme asked after a pause.

"You go first," Irma said.

Esme leaned her head onto Irma's shoulder.

"Now me," Irma ordered after ten seconds.

Esme sat up and offered her shoulder to Irma, who took it for another ten seconds.

"I haven't been here since I was little girl," Irma said as she leaned back into her own space.

"Same here," Esme recalled. "I think I was about nine. Something in the single digits. Back when Christmas was everything."

"I've never seen this resort during the day," Irma realized.

"Me neither."

"I have no idea what it looks like."

"There's no reason to come here if you're not staying here."

"Maybe if it was right on the beach. The only reason we come to the coast in the daytime is for the beach."

"I've never been to the beach at night," Esme said.

They continued light-gazing.

"Shall we?" Irma asked.

Esme didn't reply. She stood up.

They didn't actually reach the beach. They parked along the ridge above the shore, walked toward the trailhead and thought better of descending it in the dark.

A narrow path lined the top, featuring a bench every fifty yards. They reached the nearest one and swapped their seat at the light show for one facing the darkness.

There was no moon. They could hear the ocean, smell its musk, feel its mist, but could hardly see it. White crests curling atop the surf were the only visible features.

Perhaps because the Philippines was somewhere on the other side, Irma asked Esme "Do you know where Dorothy works?"

"At a hospital in Bakersfield."

"Housekeeping?"

"Yes. The lawyers helped her get a phone and a place to stay. Her English is getting pretty good. At least when she texts."

Esme listened to the waves roar and wondered if Irma was going to ask if the text reference meant that she had not spoken to Dorothy since she got out of detention and started her new job.

She was planning on visiting her. She had an Economics midterm on the day Dorothy was released, then the texts from her started to arrive since she was able to start using her phone, so she felt like they were talking. The final spring semester coming up was the lightest schedule of her life. She only had three academic classes left thanks to all her summer units. Even if she got a lead role in the musical, she wouldn't have to worry about studying for much else. Leaving her sixth period free meant conceding the top of the class to Gina, but she had grown less concerned with some of her past goals over the past year.

The waves crashed beneath them as she prepared to explain this to Irma.

But she didn't ask.

And she never spoke of Dorothy again.

Whenever she and Esme spent time together from then on, they knew their days of seeing each other every day in person were numbered, so they spent the countdown reminiscing over their shared history. If they did talk about other people, it was people they had grown up with, who would also be little else but words and pictures on a screen every now and then in the future, if they were anything.

The same nostalgic pressure steered Daisy away from bringing up Dorothy as well. She only spoke of friends and rivals as their days together waned. Esme took Journalism again. Not only for a last dance with Daisy, but so she could take part in producing the Senior Edition, which featured a rundown of where everyone was headed after graduation.

That was her primary reason for a final round of Journalism, we teased her. A joke grew legs and ran through a variety of inflections about her controlling the narrative of everyone's accomplishments, not just her own. She pushed back on our heckling with a pitch for more interviews with seniors who were not going to college the following year, those from the "Joining the Workforce" and "Joining the Military" lists. The Senior Edition traditionally showcased one, maybe two of them, but she thought they deserved more attention. Daisy warned her that a lot of them don't necessarily want their decisions broadcast as loudly as the acceptance chasers. Esme interviewed a bunch of them anyway, attached to an idea that she could perhaps combine a variety of their quotes into a larger piece.

Some of us noticed that after she finished an interview, she would run it by one of the section editors and weave Dorothy and her coworkers into the exchange, utilizing their time served in The Riverbed as a flimsy springboard for her to wonder aloud if the graduating seniors with the modest plans had possibly set themselves up for a Dorothy-like existence. She still wanted to talk about her, but having burned through Daisy and Irma on the subject, she was using the students she interviewed as Dorothy substitutes.

So the rest of us on the editorial board started to hear more about her. Some of us were more receptive to the Dorothy Diaries than others. We decided it was a good way to avoid hearing about all the colleges she was considering. Esme scarcely mentioned them anymore, and we wanted to keep it that way. College had become an afterthought to her, as if she traded one obsession for another. She offered no announcements, and was reluctant to name names when asked which schools said yes. Her indecision about where she was going to commit seemed sincere. She fended us off by saying where she goes to college doesn't matter, what matters is all the time afterwards. We ended up wondering if maybe she was involved with the Senior Edition to keep her name out of it.

She used her long list of college suitors as the basis of a joke she crafted on her drive out to visit the hospital that Dorothy kept clean. If Dorothy happened to ask if she had been accepted by any of her dream schools, she would say, "Yes, no thanks to you!" as a ploy to explain how she had not used her story on the applications. Then it dawned on her that Dorothy may be hurt by the omission. Esme didn't trust herself to cross a language barrier in explaining either her rationale or her joke, so she nixed the idea.

The vacant valley that separated Esme's home from Dorothy's work was starting to bloom. The straight line of the highway split her thoughts and scattered them across the budding hills. Her mind wandered the wildflowers and oaks and she rediscovered Rafa's claim that changing the world or being part of it is a choice. She had run this idea by those closest to her, Irma and Daisy and her parents.

She was especially contemplative, as the spring semester of her senior year felt like she was retiring from a career, which led to the kind of ruminating she imagined people experienced when they really did retire: whether they had chosen the right path, whether they had been good people, whether they had mattered, whether anything did.

She echoed the consensus of those she loved, who saw Rafa's point, but ultimately decided his philosophy was a false dilemma. Change and participation could be simultaneous, but doing both led to the hardest version of each, which meant it more or less was a choice for most of us.

Wondering whether she was within that range, with most of us, or above it was another question that crept up on her during her ride through the sparse countryside. She wasn't below the norm. She was convinced of that. And while standing atop the lowest bar didn't prove much, it was a reliable source of comfort. "If you can't reach the top, piss on the bottom," her crotchety grandpa might say if she had a crotchety grandpa. None of her grandparents had yet to age out of their filters. They still cared about what people thought of them.

For her meeting with Dorothy, all she needed to be was average. What mattered most was being there. The mission was simple.

Esme didn't tell her she was visiting that particular day. She had asked Dorothy about her schedule, and when she went on breaks.

Dorothy told her the days and hours, then texted "Are you coming to see me?"

Her choice of words, asking if she was coming to see her, drove Esme to recognize that she had already seen Dorothy, and heard her, but never touched her, never so much as put a hand on her shoulder.

Esme said, "Yes, I'm taking the trip soon."

Dorothy replied with a happy face emoji.

Esme never cared for emojis. She took some pride in having a way with words. Proud enough to feel protective of them, but she didn't keep watch with any aggression. Her restraint was grounded in a pesky ambivalence about her talent. She appreciated it, but often wished the same level of ability had emerged in some other area, like music or sports, something more obvious to the world and perceived as less pretentious.

She also learned early in life that most words disappear. The books on her shelves were all familiar, she knew the stories, but not the words. Her father and mother offered plenty of encouraging words, but she could not quote them. She once told her father that a certain pep talk he was giving her one night wasn't helpful. She couldn't remember what the talk was about. But she remembered his reaction. Rather than being upset with her or himself, he smiled and said he was filling the air with words to prove he was trying, that the effort provided comfort, and the language was incidental.

She was paraphrasing, but confident she captured the spirit of the moment.

The feeling of that memory was all she needed in the parking lot of the hospital as she waited for Dorothy's break to start. She worried less about what to say and wondered instead if she should go in for a hug, or shake her hand.

There were no signs she could follow. The public didn't need to know the location of the employee break room. The woman at the front desk didn't know where it was. The trio of women at the nurses' station directed her to a room, but it was for medical staff. She asked a janitor where he took his breaks. He put aside his work, led her down the hall, through two turns, then stood at the end of another hall that extended from the third turn and counted the number of doors on the left she needed to pass before reaching the right place. She thanked him and found the door, which was unmarked.

Dorothy was inside, sitting at a table by herself under the fluorescent lights, eating from a cup of instant noodles.

She saw Esme and rose from her chair as though ready for a fight, leaving her spoon in the cup and approaching at a brisk pace with the usual resigned look on her face. Esme was startled at how quickly Dorothy was upon her. She didn't have a chance to decide whether to hug or shake.

The choice was never hers to make.

Dorothy grabbed her and squeezed hard, burying her face in Esme's shoulder. It reminded Esme of one of those hugs that happens outdoors in a pouring rain. Every couple of seconds Dorothy shook her arms as if to make sure her grip was secure. As the hug persisted, however, Esme imagined the shivering was an assurance, Dorothy's way of telling her she deserved it, for Esme felt otherwise.

When their embrace ended, Esme wobbled and caught her balance. Dorothy stared at her with a ferocity meant to bear her gratitude. Esme could not hold her gaze. She looked away. The ground had finally shifted, like she always wanted, but by chance, and her audience was Dorothy. Nobody else knew.

Esme was someplace else now, somewhere past good deeds that were accidental or on an application, where she was determined to earn this gratitude she could not accept.

Meanwhile she was still in the dim break room avoiding eye contact with Dorothy. Stories rarely concern themselves with what happens after the embrace in the rain, the hand shake as the victory celebration rages on in the background, the knowing look exchanged before the car window rolls up or the elevator doors shut, so Esme didn't know what to do in the immediate aftermath of her revelation, which had been building for some time. It merely reached its peak that day in Dorothy's arms.

Dorothy's conversational English was still slow. Texting made it look better because she had those extra seconds to think about her words or look them up. And Esme had not learned any Ilocano, so they went ahead and composed texts in person and instead of sending them, read them aloud to each other.

"You make your choice for college?"

"No," which didn't need a text prompter. "Not yet."

"What are you going to study?"

"Maybe International Relations."

She explained that major by looking it up on one of the college websites and showing it to Dorothy. Within seconds of scanning the page, which included stock photos of diverse young actors overplaying their roles as students from different backgrounds pretending to talk to one another, Dorothy burst out laughing. A rare case where the explanation was better than the joke.

"Maybe I can go to college," Dorothy said.

"That would be great."

"Study hotel management."

She had one-upped Esme, with no explanation necessary.

They settled into exchanging updates like when they texted from afar, which for the most part involved mundane details. As exhilarating as it was to receive an epiphany about life, it could only inform so much of the time that followed. There were still groceries to buy, clothes to fold, family members and friends to complain about, and otherwise boring stories to share that may be of interest to a precious few people in our lives, if they're in the mood to hear them.

Esme and Dorothy shared their uninteresting stories, found them fascinating, and said they would try to keep in touch. They said they would try, because they knew it was going to be difficult, that it was unrealistic, but didn't want to say so. Their lives were on different paths. Dorothy had a direction, Esme had a trajectory, and both were moving at high speed, taking them away from the place where they met, even as they sat at a table where they talked about nothing much.

Esme felt the rate of separation slow when she started to move. Walking back down the hall, through the lobby, and across the parking lot, the memory of being with Dorothy in person was already building an anchor she suspected would grow heavier with distance, and provide more weight than any virtual exchange they may have in the future.

The drive home surprised her with how light it felt to have that kind of anchor, how much higher and faster she could go in knowing someone by accident who raised the possibility there are no accidents. Thinking of this while behind the wheel of a car made her smile, and pay far more attention to the world speeding past.

# Also by Sean Boling

**The Current Mr. Orr**
Devin's Best Afterlife
Once in Two Lifetimes
Revenge and Wellness in the Sweet Hereafter

**Standalone**
Cut Flowers
Abraham the Anchor Baby Terrorist
Pigs and Other Living Things
The Summer of Our Foreclosure
Satellite Campus
A Charter to That Other Place
The Latest Version of My Love Story
Show Them What They Won
The Name Field
Should
Moral Adjacent
Over Here We Have

# About the Author

Sean lives with his family in Templeton, California. He teaches English at Cuesta College.